D0891742

The 92nd Tiger

MICHAEL GILBERT

The 92nd Tiger

HARPER & ROW, PUBLISHERS

New York / Evanston / San Francisco / London

A JOAN KAHN–HARPER NOVEL OF ADVENTURE

Library of Congress Cataloging in Publication Data

Gilbert, Michael Francis, 1912–
   The 92nd tiger.
   "A Joan Kahn-Harper novel of adventure"
   I. Title.
PZ3.G37367Ni3   [PR6013.I3335]   823'.9'14   73–4148
ISBN 0–06–011533–5

For there is an upstart crow, beautified with our feathers that, with his tiger's heart wrapped in a player's hide, supposes he is as well able to bombast out a blank verse as the best of you.

—Robert Greene, *The Groatsworth of Wit Bought with a Million of Repentance*

Part One / Personnel

Chapter 1 / The 91st Tiger

The Tiger stared down at the girl who knelt on the pile of sacking beside him. His shirt, ripped down the back, showed his magnificent dorsal muscles. A blue-black bruise, yellowing at the center, disfigured the left side of his handsome face, but his eyes were keenly alive.

"You realize what they plan to do to us?" he said.

"Yes."

"They will shoot us as soon as it is light."

"If they shoot us, I shall be happy."

The girl was small but well built. She was dressed in a loose wraparound garment. From her face and accent she could have been Burmese or Malaysian. Her name was Lai-lo Padme, or Unspotted Lotus.

"Odd thing to be happy about," said the Tiger.

"I am afraid they will torture us first."

"They will do neither. Because when they come for us we shall not be here."

"How can we get out? There is a sentry who passes this door every ten minutes. He looks in. But he has his orders. He will not come in."

"If he saw you naked, might he not come in?"

Lai-lo Padme appeared to consider the matter. She said, "If he cannot see you, he will guess that you are hiding behind the door and he will not come in, even if he sees me naked."

"That's the whole point. He *will* see me. Or he'll think he sees me. I shall be lying in the corner, on my face. He will think I have passed out after that last beating."

"How do you mean, he will think he sees you? I don't understand."

"Because I am going to take all my clothes off, too. There is plenty of straw. We can make a dummy lifelike enough to deceive him in this light."

"We could try it, I suppose," said the Unspotted Lotus doubtfully.

"Now here's where we cut," said the producer. "We'll have the dummy just off camera. It can be pushed into position. There's no difficulty about you, Hugo. You just take off your shirt and trousers. You'll be wearing bathing trunks underneath. Remember to keep your right side to the camera as much as possible. We want to highlight those bruises and scars. It's Jenny we've got to be careful about. If we don't get the camera angles dead right, we'll have those old telephones getting red hot."

"If I take this thing off," said Jenny, speaking in an accent which was suddenly more Merseyside than Malaysian, "they'll see everything down to my navel. You realize I'll have to be made up down to the hips?"

"That's the least of our worries," said the producer. "We can't have any frontal view at all. Not on a show that comes out at seven-thirty. We start with number one camera, on your back. O.K., Jack?"

"What have two and three got that I haven't?" said the number one cameraman, who had red hair and a reputation for wit.

"We cut the frame off just above the hips. Then, when we cue in the guard on three, you start turning, quite slowly, Jenny, and we pick up a half front view on number two. And when I say half front, I mean rather less than half front."

"One tit and you're oot," said Jack.

"That's quite enough from you," said the producer. He was making notes on his script. "We'll need a two-shot on three when Hugo gives the guard a karate chop. Two, you'll have to track up quite close to the door, or you'll block the sound boom."

"If I get too close to the door," said the number two cameraman, "I shan't be able to pan round and follow Hugo out."

4

The producer considered the matter. Number two was an experienced operator and didn't make unnecessary difficulties. He said, "If we angle the shot slightly, there should be room for both of you. It'll be a squeeze." He took a piece of chalk from his pocket and drew two lines on the floor.

"What about keeping the mike further back?"

"No. We want it close in when Hugo hits the guard. Viewers nowadays know all about karate chops. They like to hear them as well as see them. All right, everyone. I'm going upstairs. We'll give it a dry run first time."

"I wish they'd heat these bloody studios properly," said the Unspotted Lotus.

"It's no good, Sam," said Philippa Hayes-Borton. "It's just not on. It's not that I'm against it personally. In fact, I'm on your side. You know how I had to fight to get the last thirteen for you."

"The last series got good ratings."

"They've all had good ratings. From number one down to number seven."

"Then why not keep on with it?"

"I'll tell you why, Sam. It's because television's growing up. And people are growing up with it. Nowadays, they've got to feel themselves involved. This Tiger character lives in a dream world."

"Most people live in dream worlds," said Sam. He realized that he was up against it, but he wasn't going to give up without a fight. His private opinion of Philippa Hayes-Borton was that she was a bitch. And not even an attractive bitch, with her square face and her gray hair, which seemed to be tinged at the edges with yellow from the countless cigarettes she smoked. But since she was head of series, she had to be played up to. And Sam, as an agent, had to do most of the playing up. It was how he earned his ten percent.

He said, "In a balanced program there's room for all sorts."

"Do you think I haven't told them that? I like Hugo. He's a good actor. And he's got a big following. It's the series that's wrong, not him."

"Suppose we told the scriptwriters to update the series."

Miss Hayes-Borton shook her heavy head so emphatically that her swinging gray hair nearly knocked the cigarette out of her mouth.

She said, "You're talking nonsense, Sam. And you know it. Look. We've had—how many? Seven times thirteen. Ninety-one episodes. That means Tiger has rescued ninety-one beautiful girls and knocked out ninety-one villains. Mostly foreigners. There's hardly a member of the United Nations hasn't contributed at least one villain. The series is set hard. Set in concrete. If you tried to modernize it, you'd crack it wide open."

Sam didn't bother to argue with this, because he knew it was true. Like the seasoned campaigner he was, he shifted his ground and said, "What do you suggest?"

"I've been thinking about it. The trouble is, Hugo's an awkward age. Getting on for forty."

"Thirty-seven."

"Thirty-eight next month." She had it all down on the paper in front of her. "He's not quite old enough for father of a problem family. We've got one or two series of that sort on the drawing board."

Sam shuddered. He said, "Teen-age children. The pill. Student revolt. Pot. Generation gap. Inability to communicate. Do people really *want* that sort of thing after supper?"

"Whether they want it or not, they're going to get it. It's the company's new image."

"I think it's mad," said Sam. "Real life is so bloody nowadays that no one wants it on the screen as well. If you have to live on stew all day, you don't want it served up cold in the evening."

"We have got other slots. Has Hugo ever thought about the classics? We're doing Trollope this autumn. A lot of good supporting characters in Trollope."

"Hugo isn't a supporting character," said Sam. "He's a star."

As he said it, he seemed to be speaking some sort of epitaph.

Hugo went down in the lift with Geoffrey Larrimore, a big

middle-aged man running comfortably to fat. Geoffrey had featured in most of the Tiger episodes. He played the big wheel, the man who spent his working day in a comfortable office, dispatching other men on dangerous assignments.

As they crossed the entrance hall, George, the one-armed receptionist, said, "Good night, Mr. Larrimore. Good night, Mr. Greest. I'm sorry we shan't be having any more of the Tiger. My family all looked forward to it."

"If you've heard that," said Hugo, "you've heard more than I have."

"George always gets things in advance," said Larrimore. "I believe he's got all the conference rooms wired for sound."

"Well, I hope it's wrong, sir. It was only a buzz."

"Your buzzes are never wrong," said Hugo.

As they stepped out of the television building, a group of boys who had been waiting in the shadows hurried forward, holding autograph books in front of them but saying nothing. Each one wore, in his buttonhole or pinned to his coat, the dull bronze tiger's head which was the badge of the Tiger Fan Club.

Hugo scribbled his name on each page as it was offered to him. He had devised a special signature, with a flourish at the end that looked like a tiger's tail. Each boy, as his book was signed, muttered a word which might have been anything at all and slid off into the darkness.

"What do you suppose they do with them?" said Larrimore.

"I've often wondered," said Hugo. "One boy—I recognized him because he had a terrific squint—I must have signed his book twenty times."

"Perhaps he used them as swaps. One actor for two politicians."

"Or three actors for one soccer player. I want a drink. What about it?"

"Twist my arm hard enough and I'll come with you."

The bar was not more than half full. The proprietor recognized Hugo and gave him the big smile he reserved for ranking television personalities. The wall behind the bar was papered with signed photographs, place of honor being reserved for the proprietor shaking hands with Bob Hope. He served them himself and they took their glasses to a table in the corner.

"Do you think George is right?" Larrimore asked. "I hadn't heard anything definite."

"George is always right." Hugo finished his first whisky quickly and fetched two more. "I haven't heard anything myself, but I know Sam's having a heart-to-heart with la Hayes-Borton this evening."

"Why they wanted to make that cow head of series passes my feeble comprehension. If ever there was a man's job, I should have thought that was it."

"I don't know. They say that nearly three-quarters of the viewers are women."

"Exactly. That's why they need a man to cater to them. I'm going to get myself a sandwich. The corned beef and pickle are rather good."

They ate corned beef and pickle sandwiches with their third drinks. The room was filling up now. Larrimore lit a cigarette, said, "I smoke too much," in the tone of voice of someone who hasn't the slightest intention of stopping, and, "Just one more, if you insist," when Hugo looked at their empty glasses. "Only more water in mine this time."

When Hugo came back with the drinks, he had to push his way through the crowd. Quite a few of them were minor characters from the studios, who grinned at him. The rest were locals from the down-at-heels part of London in which, for no logical reason, the great television complex had sprung up. The two elements had not fused together very well, and there was a town-and-gown hostility which flared up from time to time.

"If George is right," said Hugo, returning to the subject which was on both their minds, "what are you going to do about it?"

"What I'd like to do is a season in rep. But that's what almost everyone wants when he gets slung out of television, so I don't suppose I shall get it. Failing that, I'm going to have a shot at this Trollope lark. I've always fancied myself as an archdeacon."

"It's all very well for you," said Hugo. "You've got plenty of options. I'm stuck. To the public, I'm the Tiger. If I turned up as the curate at Barchester, they'd think it was a gag."

"Sam will work the oracle."

"Sam Maxfeldt's a bloody good agent. He saved my bacon when I got into the top line. I made the mistake everyone makes when that happens to them. Stop me if I'm boring you."

"When I get bored, I yawn. When you see me yawning, you can stop. Not till then."

"Well, you know how it is. For a long time, even if you get the breaks, you're lucky to make more than a thousand a year."

"You're bloody lucky if you make that."

"Then, for no particular reason, you go clear up through the stratosphere and make twenty thousand."

"Go on. I like hearing about it."

"And that's when the trouble starts. The first year, you spend it. Every gorgeous penny of it. The second year, you spend most of it, but you've got a niggling feeling that you ought to put something by. The third year, you wake up. The dream's over. That's when you have to pay tax on the previous year *and* surtax on the year before. And you haven't got it."

"So what do you do?"

"Well, there's several things you can do. You can shoot yourself, or file your bankruptcy petition—or put yourself into Sam's hands and do exactly what he tells you. For the next three years, I never touched a penny of what I earned. It all went straight to Sam, and he doled me out a weekly allowance. I gave up my flat in Albany, my Jack Barclay Bentley, and about six clubs. I stopped buying a new suit every week and I went home to share a house with Mother. It was like coming off a drug jag. I didn't like it, but it's beginning to work. Sam got the tax people off my back, and one more Tiger series would have cleared me. That's why it's such a bore they have to stop right now. Time for another?"

He squeezed his way slowly back to the bar and Larrimore watched him go. A professional himself, he knew exactly what Hugo was up against. His reputation and fame were great, but they were very flimsy. They rested on one successful series. To

9

the public, he was the Tiger. The hero of ninety-one half-hour episodes. Easy to view, and easy to forget. The steep bit of the road lay ahead. The road that led to real stardom. Top billing, a choice of good parts, the center table at the Garrick Club, the New Year's Honors. Between these delectable uplands and the deceptive foothills of television popularity there was a great gulf. A gulf full of hero's friends and heroine's fathers, comic uncles, wedding guests, and second murderers.

Hugo arrived back with most of the whisky he had been carrying still in the glasses. He said, "You look bloody solemn all of a sudden, Geoff."

"I've been thinking about life."

"A mistake. Keep your mind firmly on fantasy. It's the only safe course. Cheers!"

One of the group standing near them had been staring at Hugo for some time. He was a thick-set, red-faced character with sloping shoulders and a barrel of a chest. He said, "Well, well, well. Do my eyes deceive me, or is it the old Tiger himself?"

He edged his way forward until he was standing shoulder to shoulder with Hugo, who put down his drinks and smiled politely.

"I always wanted to meet you. I seen those things you do, like karate and things like that, and I often thought, I bet he fakes 'em. I bet the other chap falls down. Right?"

"That's right."

"And I thought to myself, suppose he came up against someone his own size and weight. Someone like me, f'rinstance. Who'd win then, f'rinstance?"

"I've no idea," said Hugo.

"Care to try?"

"Certainly not."

"Yellow as well?"

One of the man's friends said, "Lay off, Cliff. You're tight."

"Not too tight to take a poke at this big phony."

The swing came so slowly that Hugo had no difficulty in avoiding it. The only thing it upset was the table. As the glasses

10

on it hit the floor, the landlord and one of his assistants arrived, splitting the crowd like tanks going through undergrowth. They got the red-faced man by an arm each, holding him with one hand behind the elbow and the other by his collar, which they twisted until they choked him. Then they ran him to the door. A path opened before them. One of the bystanders opened the door. The red-faced man disappeared through it with a lovely crash. The landlord came back and said, "I'm sorry about that, sir. Get that broken glass swept up, Ted. We don't want anyone hurt. I'll fetch you two more drinks."

"Don't bother," said Hugo. "We're going."

When they got outside, the red-faced man had disappeared.

Larrimore said, "Do you often get trouble like that?"

"Every now and then," said Hugo. He sounded very tired suddenly.

The house he shared with his mother was on the river above Richmond. She had the ground floor, on account of her legs, and he had the rest of it. It was a nice house, with a garden down to the river and a view of Eel-Pie Island, and was worth three times what he had given for it five years before.

When he got there, all the ground-floor lights were out and he let himself in quietly. On the hall table there was a single letter, which must have come with the afternoon post. The envelope was buff, and square, and he thought at first that it was a tax demand, but it wasn't.

The letter inside was from the Foreign Office, Whitehall, and was dated that day.

It invited Mr. Hugo Greest to call at the Foreign Office on the following afternoon, at two-thirty if convenient, and ask for a Mr. Taverner.

Chapter 2 / Mr. Taverner of the Foreign Office

There were three gray-haired ladies. They sat, like judges in the Court of Appeal, side by side at the broad counter that blocked one end of the spacious entrance hall. Behind them, frosted glass windows obscured what would otherwise have been a view of Downing Street. From the wall on their left a gentleman in full court dress looked down at them.

Fine film set, thought Hugo. A party of terrorists set out to kidnap the Foreign Secretary. Three of them leap the counter and overpower the secretaries. In the film they would be younger, of course, and much prettier—

"Can I help you?" said the central lady sharply.

"I beg your pardon," said Hugo. "I have an appointment with Mr. Taverner. The Arabian Department."

"Fill out this form, please."

Hugo studied the pink form. Some of it was easy. His name. He could do that. And the date. But what about "Nature of business"?

"I'm afraid," he said, "that I've no idea what the nature of my business is."

The central lady looked at him with increased suspicion. She said, "You must have some idea."

"I'm afraid not. You see, I got a letter asking me to call. Mr. Taverner didn't say what it was about."

"That's very unusual," said the right-hand lady.

"Perhaps you could ring him up and ask him what he wants to see me about. Then I could put it on the form."

"We can't do that," said the left-hand lady. "If you weren't told what you were here for, it's probably confidential, you see."

It was a deadlock.

The right-hand lady, who seemed to be the most helpful of the three, had an idea. She said, "Why don't you put 'Business'?"

This seemed a neat solution. The bench considered it and concurred.

In the space opposite the word "Business" Hugo wrote "Business." The form was then passed back over the counter, approved by the Court of Appeal, and handed to a veteran of the Crimean War who had hobbled up.

"Follow me, sir," said the veteran.

Hugo followed him. Into a lift, out of the lift, along a short passage, into a much longer passage. The veteran was in no hurry. After a hundred years of combat, he had come to rest in this dim but comfortable mansion, full of enormous faded portraits and lined with cupboards full of documents which were once secret topped by bookshelves of unreadable and unread reports. The ghosts of an imperial past moved softly ahead of them, prowling down the corridors, lurking in the galleries, whispering in the shadows.

A long time later, they came to a door. The veteran knocked at it and a polite voice bade them enter. The veteran entered, laid the pink form on the edge of the desk, saluted, and withdrew, closing the door softly behind him.

"So glad you could come, Mr. Greest," said Taverner. He was tall, and thin, and appeared to be dressed for a funeral. "Let me take your coat." He took Hugo's raincoat and suspended it from an apparatus like a small gallows which stood behind the door. While he was doing so, Hugo took stock of the room.

It was a narrow room, so narrow that in its original design it might have been a passage. A strip of Oriental carpet covered some of the floor. The rest was brown linoleum. A tiny coal fire smoldered in the old-fashioned grate. The furniture was waiting-room mahogany. It was not at all his idea of an appropriate room for the head of the Arabian Department. A television

13

producer, even on a minimum budget, would not have considered it.

"You must have been surprised to get my note," said Mr. Taverner.

"Well, I was a bit."

"It's not a very usual situation. The fact is that I have a rather unusual proposition to put to you. I thought it would be easier if I explained it to you personally. You'll certainly need time to think about it. It's so unusual that I shouldn't be at all surprised if you rejected it out of hand."

His tone of voice suggested that not only would he be unsurprised, he would actually be glad if his proposition was rejected. Hugo said, "Let's hear about it before we turn it down."

"I have to offer you the post of military adviser to the ruler of Umran."

"Come again."

"Umran, in the Persian Gulf. I don't expect you've heard of it. Not many people have." Mr. Taverner unfolded himself from behind his desk, moved across to the wall, and pulled a cord. A map descended from a mahogany valance.

"There it is," he said. "It needs a large-scale map to show it at all. It's the very tip of the peninsula. Its nearest neighbor is Ras al Khaima."

Hugo peered at the map with interest.

"All that green bit on the right," he said. "That's Muscat and Oman, isn't it?"

"The Sultanate of Oman. It changed its name after the palace coup last year."

"And those bits down there?"

"Umm al-Qaiwain, Fujaira, Ajman and Sharja. They're all independent trucial sheikdoms. Interesting places. They live in hopes of striking it rich when oil is discovered."

"And Umran?"

"Umran had what you might call a mixed economy. As you see, it is less than fifty miles across the straits to Iran."

"The Gibraltar of the Persian Gulf."

Mr. Taverner considered the expression, repeating it silently to himself.

14

"Yes," he said. "You might call it that. It was not the political significance of its position that I was considering when I mentioned its nearness to Iran, although that has important implications. What I meant to imply was that its proximity to the mainland on the other side made it a natural entrepôt for smuggling. Gold smuggling in particular. Its other principal source of income was the striking of new and remarkable issues of postage stamps. There is one set in which the head of the ruler was printed upside down which is in demand by philatelists all over the world."

"You say that these *were* its sources of income. Do I gather that they have now struck oil?"

"They have not actually struck it. Like all those states, they have sold exploration concessions to hopeful prospectors. Sometimes the same concession several times over. But there are now more exciting possibilities. A company called Metbor, who drill for hard minerals in most parts of the world, are examining a number of trial borings in Umran at the moment."

"What do they expect to find? Gold? Silver? Copper?"

Mr. Taverner pursed his lips and said, "Yes, that sort of thing."

He's lying, said Hugo to himself. I wonder why. He thought that the moment had come to ask the question. It had to be asked sooner or later.

"Why pick on me?"

Mr. Taverner smiled faintly. "As you may imagine, this was the first question which we asked. We were very willing to assist the ruler and we had available a number of most suitable candidates. Men who had spent a good deal of time in that part of the world, with experience in the services or in diplomacy. We compiled a short list of six of the most promising and invited the ruler to interview them and select one. He rejected them."

"All of them?"

"All of them, and without even seeing them. He wanted you."

"He must be mad."

Mr. Taverner appeared to be considering the point very carefully. He said, "Not mad. Romantic. He is also a student of

15

television. He has observed you, on a number of occasions, dealing with difficult and dangerous situations. He feels—and there we must agree with him—that there is likely to be no shortage of difficulties and dangers in Umran in the near future. And he has decided that you are the man he would like to have with him."

"I suppose he realizes that success on the screen is a lot easier than success in real life."

"Subconsciously I think he does. But your repeated triumphs . . . How many, by the way?"

"Ninety-one."

"Yes. Ninety-one. They have had a sort of cumulative effect. He even has the impression, which he gained from an incident in which you temporarily impersonated a drunken Arab camel driver, that you speak fluent Arabic. We tried to explain to him that you would have been coached in the few words you had to speak, and that this was the extent of your knowledge."

"If you explained that to him, you were off beam."

"Oh?"

"I haven't always been an actor, you know. In fact, I came to it comparatively late. I studied Oriental languages at Cambridge. When I left, my first job was as secretary to the late Professor Emil van der Hoetzen. I expect you've heard of him?"

"Indeed, yes."

"I spent three years with him in the Middle East. Mostly under canvas in the desert near Homs. I won't say that I became a classical Arabist, but I was quite capable of holding my own in a slanging match with a camel driver."

"I see. Well, that certainly makes a difference."

"But not very much?"

"Frankly, no. To handle the problems which are bound to arise, we should have wished that you had had some diplomatic training. Or failing that, some military experience. You were too young to have been in the war, I suppose."

"Much too young. I even missed the call-up. But why would military experience have been useful? Are you expecting a war in those parts?"

"Not a world war. But a private war. Yes. In fact, I should say there are more excuses for starting a private war in that particular area than anywhere else in the world. Iraq and Iran are still capable of going to war over the Shatt-al-Arab. There are endless causes of dispute over the median lines which divide the continental shelf. In the old days, when the sea bed only produced pearl oysters, it was tricky enough. Now it produces oil. Iraq covets Kuwait. Saudi Arabia wants the Buraimi Oasis. And finally, there are the Tumbs."

"Didn't Iran grab them the other day?"

"Correct. But they are not the only islands. Not by any means. In fact, there is a chain of tiny islands—sandspits really—off the coast of Umran. You spoke a moment ago of Umran being in the same position as Gibraltar. Can you visualize the sort of difficulties which might arise if the Straits of Gibraltar were somewhat wider and there were a number of uninhabited islands in the middle?"

"It sounds tricky, certainly. By the way, who owns these islands?"

"According to us, Ras al Khaima. According to Iran, Iran. And now the ruler of Umran has himself staked a claim. It is based, as far as we can make out, both on physical propinquity and on archaeological grounds. He claims to have discovered the tomb of the founder of his family, the Ferini, on the largest of them."

Hugo said, "I can understand that there might be a shooting war between Iran—who have, I understand, got a sizable army —and one of the Western powers, if they chose to stick up for —which was it?—Ras al Khaima. But I can't quite see tiny little Umran making an impression on either side. How many of them are there?"

"At the last census, about eight thousand. But that was five years ago. There are probably ten thousand by now. It's not the numbers that matter. It's the people. The Al Ferini are desert Arabs. Their male children are taught to handle firearms at an early age. If they are provoked, they will shoot. They are fighters."

As Mr. Taverner said this, he gave a very tiny sigh. His one

17

window looked out over a corner of Horse Guards Parade. The rain, which had been threatening all morning, had started to come down hard. Pedestrians were scurrying for shelter. But it was not this which made him sigh. Mr. Taverner was a member of the East India Club and in his lunch hours, when the weather was fine, he liked to walk there, across the park, up Waterloo Place and across Pall Mall to St. James's Square. In the club, which was one of the last relics of the raj, were numerous portraits. They were portraits of men who had brought peace and progress to a warring and primitive subcontinent. Sir Henry Lawrence and Arthur Phayre. The incomparable Bubs. The black-bearded John Nicholson, who had threatened to shoot his own general if he refused to order an attack. They, too, were fighters. Were there any left? Could a nation of fighters lose its martial spirit within a mere hundred years? It had happened before. Rome had gone soft in less than a century. That man in front of him. What good could he possibly achieve? He was not a soldier. He was an actor. Probably a pansy. Most actors were pansies, or so he understood.

He became aware that the silence had gone on rather a long time, and said, "I expect you have a lot of questions you'd like to ask."

"One, certainly," said Hugo. "You've mentioned these possibilities and dangers. Why should they worry us? We've cleared out of the Gulf, haven't we?"

"Politically."

"And militarily."

"Not entirely. We are retaining certain airfields as staging posts for the RAF, and the navy will pay courtesy visits from time to time. Also we have agreed to continue training the Oman Scouts. Broadly I agree. Our main forces have gone. But that is far from being the whole picture. We still have very considerable commercial interests. In spite of recent discoveries in the North Sea, nearly two-thirds of the oil available to the noncommunist world comes from the Gulf. And half of it is ours."

"Then I think we were crazy to take the army away."

18

Mr. Taverner smiled his diplomatic smile and said, "The decision did not rest with this office, Mr. Greest. But I can tell you this. If any man, in any position, is able to use what influence he has toward maintaining peace and the status quo, and allowing the oil to flow through the pipe lines and the tankers to pass freely, he would not find the government ungrateful. Of that I am sure."

C.M.G., thought Hugo, maybe a K.C.M.G. Well, that would be something to show them at Television Center. He said, "I'd want time to think about it."

"Of course."

"What would you suggest would be the next step?"

"I think you ought to have a word with the ruler. He is staying at the Dorchester. Since his visit to this country is unofficial, he has registered under the name of Mr. Smith."

Chapter 3 / Sheik Ahmed bin Rashid al Ferini

"Mr. Smith, sir?" said the receptionist at the Dorchester, consulting a list. "Which Mr. Smith would that be?"

"He's an Arabian gentleman."

"That would be Sheik Ahmed of Umran, I expect."

"Right," said Hugo. He wondered who all the other Mr. Smiths were.

"I'll ring up and tell him you're here, Mr. Greest. Would you like to wait in the reception hall?"

Hugo retired to one of the comfortable chairs provided by the Dorchester for its visitors and sank back into it. Since leaving the Foreign Office, he had spent a busy two hours. First he had called on Sam Maxfeldt in his untidy little office near Covent Garden. Sam had confirmed the rumor that there was no immediate prospect of an eighth series of the Tiger, and had listened impassively to an account of Hugo's visit to the Foreign Office.

"If it's a temporary job," he said, "it might be a good idea. Producers are like cats. Make approaches to them and they're not interested. Ignore them and they're all over you. If I let it be known that you're not available at any price for six months, their mouths'll start watering."

"It didn't sound to me like a six-month job."

"How long?"

"We haven't fixed up any details yet. But two or three years, I imagine."

"Then you mustn't do it. No one can be off the stage for three years and come back. If it's three years, it's permanent."

"Would that be a bad thing?"

Sam reflected.

"For you, or me, or the great British public?"

"Let's keep the great British public out of it."

"For me, certainly it would be bad. You're a valuable property. For you—I don't know. That Hayes-Borton woman put her finger on it when she said you were an awkward age. If this Tiger thing hadn't been so bloody successful, I'd have had you doing all the things that really count. Repertory, and small parts at the Old Vic and Stratford, and maybe a film. As it is, you're a one-man band, and when the band stops playing . . ."

He spread his arms expressively.

"You mean I'm through."

"No. I don't mean that. I could name half a dozen people who've climbed out of situations like this and are now respectable pillars of the stage. What I'm saying is, it's a hard climb. Six months away won't hurt. Particularly if you really are doing a job, not sitting at home waiting for the telephone to ring."

"Maybe I won't even last six months. It sounds a rocky sort of berth."

"You'd better have a word with Jim Lewis. He'll put you wise to the tax angles."

So Hugo had gone off next to consult Jim Lewis. In ancient times, he reflected, if a man was starting out on a dangerous journey overseas, he would consult the astrologers and the priests. Now he went to see his tax accountant. . . .

He became aware that someone was standing in front of him. It was a small brown man in a blue suit. The only thing remarkable about him was his tie, which looked like an impressionist's idea of a sun setting in a stormy sea.

He said, "Mr. Greest? Sayyed Nawaf-al-Elkan, Head of Finance. I am pleased to see you here. I will take you up to His Highness."

He spoke excellent English and had an attractive smile. On the way up in the lift, he said, in Arabic, "The ruler has with him only his eldest son, Hussein, myself, and two secretaries. The visit is quite informal."

Hugo said, trying out his Arabic, finding the once familiar

words coming awkwardly to his tongue, "Should I address His Highness as Mr. Smith?"

"That will not be necessary." Nawaf knocked at the door of one of the third-floor suites, which was unlocked after a moment's delay. A tall man in a djellabah, whom Hugo took to be one of the secretaries, held the door open for them and ushered them in.

His Highness Sheik Ahmed bin Rashid bin Abdullah al Ferini, ruler of Umran, was standing with his back to the window. Hugo's first impression was of a very big man with a jutting black beard. A man who entirely filled a light-gray suit, who smiled, held out his hand, and said, in English which was good, but not as accentless as Nawaf's, "Nice to see you, Mr. Greest. Please sit down. Nice weather we are having."

The secretary, who had vanished, reappeared with three cups of coffee on a tray. It was all very civilized.

When the secretary had taken himself off again, the ruler said, "Mr. Taverner, your Foreign Department, will have explained to you what I require. Will you do it?"

Until that moment, Hugo would have said that he had not made his mind up. To his surprise he found himself saying, in matter-of-fact tones, "I'll do my best."

"Excellent," said the ruler. As though this was a prearranged cue, the bedroom door on the other side of the suite opened and a boy came out.

"Allow me to introduce you to my son, Hussein."

Hugo got up and shook hands ceremonially with Hussein. It was difficult to judge his age. Hugo put him down as sixteen and found out later that he had overguessed by a year.

The boy was wearing a Norfolk jacket and gabardine trousers. His black hair was long, but no longer than that of an English boy of any age. He took his jacket off, hung it over the back of a chair, and said, "Would you think it great cheek, Mr. Greest, if I asked you to take your coat off?"

"Not a bit," said Hugo.

Could this be some custom of the Trucial Coast? Equivalent, perhaps, to removing one's shoes when entering a mosque?

22

Hussein walked round behind Hugo and said, "It was *not* a trick of the camera, Father. It is true. Look at those fine muscles in the shoulders and the back."

"Really," said the ruler, "this is no way to treat a guest. He is not a horse, to be judged by his points. Put your coat on at once and sit down."

"They said it was done by cameras and trick lighting. I knew it was not true."

"Hussein has been taking a course of physical exercises to develop his own muscles," said the ruler. "So far he has succeeded only in splitting three shirts."

Hussein said, "I saw this yesterday. Do you think it might be any good?"

He showed Hugo a page which had been torn from an American magazine. It showed a prodigious man, stripped to the waist, his fists clenched and his arms slightly bent, a posture which brought his pectoral muscles into convenient relief. Beside him drooped a thin man, with matchstick arms and a protuberant stomach.

Once I was like that, said the caption.

It seemed to be an advertisement for a chest expander.

"I know which of those two men I'd back to live to a happy old age," said Hugo.

"You think it is no use, then?"

"None of those implements are any good. They develop one particular set of muscles at the expense of all the others. When I had to put on a bit of muscle myself for the close shots, the producer sent me along to a gymnasium. I thought it would be full of wonderful gadgets, too. I was very disappointed when the instructor told me that all I had to do was lie on my back, hook my toes under a bar, and raise my trunk a hundred times. After a few weeks of that, he produced an old barbell, the sort of thing weight lifters use, but not at all heavy. I had to bend down and pick it up a hundred times. That was all there was to it. Incidentally, if you try those two exercises, do them in the right order or you'll damage yourself."

"The picking up I understand," said the boy. "But lifting your trunk . . . How was that done? You say you hooked your toes *under* a bar. If we moved that table against the wall—"

"No," said the ruler.

"It would only take a minute."

"No. Mr. Greest is here to talk business. Serious business. I have asked you to be present because it may concern you one day. Now sit down and behave yourself."

Hussein sat down. It seemed that on the Trucial Coast children occasionally obeyed their parents.

"I will tell you, Mr. Greest, just what I have it in my mind to do. You must be aware of the advantages of our geographical position in Umran. We are the central point of the hegemony of the Gulf. The fulcrum of its power. Our position is similar to that of your country at the time of your first Queen Elizabeth. In size and in population you were small. In spirit and opportunity you were great. Is that not true?"

The comparison was absurd. But the words, as spoken by this large, virile, strikingly handsome person, did not seem absurd. Sparta. Carthage. Venice. Tiny states had swayed the world before. When the mighty powers were in equal balance, the smallest weight could tip the scale.

"And why was your Queen Elizabeth so great? I have studied your history books, Mr. Greest. I know the answer. She had a fighting navy, and she was not afraid to use it. The second consideration, you understand, is the more important of the two. It is no use having a loaded pistol in your pocket if you dare not take it out and fire it. That is the position with the Western nations today. Their imposing armaments, their bombers, their submarines, even their long-range artillery are all built to carry nuclear weapons which they dare not use. That is why a handful of ragged guerrillas were able to make a long nose at the American might in Vietnam."

Hugo said, "I understand, Your Highness, that you have a people of high fighting spirit. But have you arms for them? Conventional arms, I mean."

The ruler, who had been standing, now came and sat near Hugo. On the table between them he laid a sheet of paper. It

24

was ruled with faint blue lines and looked as though it had been torn from a cheap writing pad.

He said, "It shall be your first assignment, Mr. Greest, to buy us what we require."

"He wants you to do what?" said Mr. Taverner.

"Go shopping for him. This is the list."

Rifles (magazine and automatic)

Medium and heavy machine guns

3.5" bazookas

Mortars—2" and 4"

Light and medium artillery (ranges up to 25,000 m.; on mobile mountings)

A.A. guns   (ditto)

Antitank guns   (ditto)

Ammunition for all the above

Helicopters (personnel and load carrying)

Tracked vehicles (for movement across sand)

Engineer and signaling equipment

To be sufficient for a brigade of 2,000 men divided into two motorized battalions of 600 men, each with artillery and engineer support and a helicopter detachment with ground crews

Mr. Taverner looked at the list thoughtfully.

He said, "It's going to cost a fair amount of money. Has he got it?"

"I gather that part of it's all right. He's had some news from Umran. Something about a mineral strike."

"Has he, though." Mr. Taverner made a small note on the pad in front of him. He seemed more impressed by the minerals than he had been by the armaments.

"Did he tell you what mineral had been found?" Mr. Taverner recollected his diplomatic training and added, "You mustn't tell me if you heard it in confidence, of course."

"I couldn't tell you anyway, because I didn't recognize the name. It wasn't one I'd heard before."

"Wolframite or scheelite?"

"Nothing like that."

"I see."

"What I want to know is, where am I going to buy this lot? It doesn't seem to me the sort of thing you could get at Harrods or Selfridges."

"There's no difficulty about that," said Mr. Taverner sadly. "In fact, once the news gets about that you're in the market for arms and are prepared to pay cash, the difficulty will be keeping the sellers off. If I were you, I should start with the Crown Agents."

Chapter 4 / Colonel Rex

"I think we should be able to manage most of that," said Major Gilliland.

"You mean you keep that sort of thing in stock?"

"We don't keep anything in stock. When we get an order, we buy what we can. Mainly from the Ministry of Supply. Bits and pieces from other places."

"And do you get many orders as big as this?"

The major smiled faintly and said, "Last week I had to find two destroyers."

"Good heavens," said Hugo. "I'd no idea this sort of thing went on. Where does it all come from? I suppose we finished the last war with a mass of stuff we didn't need, is that it?"

"It's not only the ending of a major war, Mr. Greest. Weapons go out of fashion almost as quickly as ladies' clothes. Take those rifles. If you were after .303 Lee Enfield No. 4's, or American M.I. Garand carbines, or AR-10's, we could let you have them at once and at a reasonable price. We could even get you M-14's or AR-15's. If, on the other hand, you were looking for something up-to-the-moment, like an M-16 or a Russian AK-47, we'd have to shop round for it, and it would cost you a lot of money."

Observing the blank look on Hugo's face, he said, "You're new to this game, aren't you?"

"To me," said Hugo, "a rifle is a thing which I remember, vaguely, from my schooldays. It was brown, it was oily, and it was infernally heavy. It had a bolt at one end and a knob to fix a bayonet on at the other. It was called, I think, a service rifle."

"And a very good weapon it was," said the major, with the first spark of enthusiasm he had shown. "The trouble is that weapons nowadays have become too sophisticated altogether."

"Any help you can give me, technical or otherwise, will be gratefully received."

"Then you've had no experience of weapons since your schooldays?"

"I've handled a lot of small arms. But they were carefully plugged Lugers and Berettas. And when I pulled the trigger, the noise was made by a sound-effects man."

"I see. Well, it's something of a jungle you're stepping into."

"So Taverner said."

"Taverner?"

"He's the man at the Foreign Office who sent me here. He said that as soon as it was known that I was in the market for arms, I'd have a crowd of people on my neck."

"It's a competitive business. It can be a very profitable one. The leaders in the field are the Americans. I saw an estimate the other day that they had sold more than fifty billion dollars' worth of arms since the last war. Of course, a billion doesn't mean quite the same on the other side of the Atlantic as it does here. But it's a pretty staggering figure all the same. The American government gets the lion's share. They've got a section in the Department of Defense which does nothing but handle sales. The ILNS. Very popular with the politicians. It's the only part of the Pentagon which makes money instead of spending it."

"But there are private operators?"

"Certainly. Cummins is the best known. He's so big he's respectable. There are others who—well, let's say they're prepared to cut a few corners to get their fingers in the gravy. Abacus and Target, for instance."

"Come again."

"Abacus is the Anglo-Bostonian Arms Corporation of the U.S. Target is Trans American Rifle and Gun Enterprises of Topeka. And there are plenty of others. Smaller and even less scrupulous ones, right down to individual wheelers and dealers. Arms are

28

big business in North America. I can't swear that it's true, but it's commonly believed that the only reason Uncle Sam wouldn't drop Taiwan, which was really a great embarrassment to them, was because the politicians were subject to such pressure from the gun lobby."

But Major Gilliland, Hugo thought, would not be a very promising subject for pressure. He was dry, thin, and indestructible, a man from whom all superfluous fat and superfluous emotion had already been squeezed.

"Where do we come in the race?"

"As arms salesmen? Difficult to say, because no figures are ever published. No reliable figures, that is. America's certainly first, by several lengths. Then Belgium, Sweden, Italy, and ourselves in a bunch would be my guess."

"And does the general public know what goes on? I mean, I'd no idea . . ."

"The facts have all been published."

"Do people approve?"

Major Gilliland smiled thinly and said, "Most of my friends know what I do. I haven't noticed any of them actually spitting."

"I didn't mean that. You're doing a job. What I meant was, ideologically. The idea of selling arms to people to kill each other with."

"I've never been able to make out what people think. At one time we believed in international arms cartels run by sinister financiers who provoked European wars for profit. It was nonsense, of course. If there's one thing that kills international profit, it's a major war. On the other hand, there's a strong theoretical argument against equipping guerrillas and rebels with modern arms."

"Theoretical?"

"Certainly. In practice it's neater and kinder to kill someone with a rifle than with a panga."

"I suppose so," said Hugo doubtfully.

"On the other hand, you could argue that to equip a state like Umran with a modern, efficiently armed force is the best guarantee against further trouble. But you came to ask about arms, not to listen to arguments. I think the next sensible step would be for me to put you in touch with someone from Ordnance who can talk over the technical details with you. It'll take a day or two to arrange."

"As long as it's only a day or two," said Hugo. "My brief acquaintance with Sheik Ahmed suggests to me that when he wants something, he doesn't want it tomorrow. He wants it the day before yesterday."

"I'll get my secretary to fix it." He must have pressed a button, because a dumpy middle-aged lady wearing pebble glasses had appeared in the room. "Give us a telephone number where we can contact you, Mr. Greest."

After some reflection, he gave them Sam Maxfeldt's telephone number. He could visualize his mother's reactions if someone rang up and told her that a consignment of four-inch mortars was ready for inspection.

At the moment when Hugo was leaving the offices of the Crown Agents on Millbank, Colonel Leroy Delmaison (Colonel Rex to his friends) was entering one of the flats in Inverness Mansions, on the north side of the Cromwell Road.

He opened the curtains, turned on one bar of the electric fire, sank down into the shabby, chintz-covered armchair, and sighed.

He was a man to whom, in or out of uniform, the word "dapper" would seem appropriate. The remains of his reddish brown hair was dressed neatly round his sun-browned shining baldpate. A reddish-brown mustache jutted, in the appropriate cavalry officer manner, from his upper lip. The hair on each side of his face had been prolonged, and partly concealed the fact that his right ear was missing and the right side of his face was scarred. Part of his jawbone was missing, too. A section made of silver had been inserted after the explosion which had removed his right ear.

Like most people who travel a lot, the colonel disliked hotels. Small unpretentious hotels, medium-sized family hotels, huge and splendid international hotels—he had tried them all many

30

times and had found them, for different reasons, distasteful. It had been with gratitude, therefore, that he had accepted a friend's offer of this flat for a few weeks. It was a bachelor's apartment. Shabby covers and curtains, books on the shelves, drink in the corner cupboard, and a double bed, in case your tastes ran to company at night.

Colonel Rex sighed again. Mixed with the satisfaction was an element of regret.

The colonel was a man who had trained himself to observe. He had therefore not overlooked the young man in the neat suit with the sallow-skinned, almost hairless face who had been sitting doing nothing in particular in the arrival lounge at Heath Row; and who, in the company of a second young man, so like him that he might have been his brother, had followed the colonel from Heath Row to the flat.

The colonel had been driving a fast car, and he knew all the clever side roads and byways down which a driver might switch and double, but because he had learned the first rule of being followed, he had made no attempt to use them. (Don't try to throw off your followers. Lead them quietly to wherever it is you happen to be going. Let them see you park your car and go inside. Let them discover that this is your base. Then they will be happy to watch it. *And you can watch them.* Until you are ready to deal with them.)

There were a number of possible reasons for the young men being there. The slightly splayed nostrils, the neat rounded countersunk ears, and the color and texture of the hair suggested a point of origin in the Antilles where Spaniard mixed with Indian. Haitian, Dominican, or Puerto Rican? Puerto Ricans, the colonel considered, were the most single-minded assassins in the world. In 1950 they had a near miss at President Truman and four years later had opened fire in the House of Representatives and wounded five congressmen. On the latter occasion, the attempt had been made with weapons supplied by the colonel, who had, in the past decade, concluded many profitable deals in that part of the world. One, in particular, had held the seeds of future trouble.

He had sold to the army of a small but proud republic five

hundred revolvers. They had new shiny black grips and handsome lanyards and were invoiced as Smith & Wesson .455 revolvers at fifteen pounds each. And there was no doubt that the chamber of the revolver accepted a .455 bullet. They also carried the indisputable mark of the Birmingham Proofing House to show that they had stood up to the rigorous tests which that body imposes.

What had not been made clear to the purchasers was that at the time when they had passed the proofing house, they had been .45's. The extra .005 of metal had been reamed out of them in the colonel's own workshop in Quebec City.

It is true that by removing .005 of metal, the colonel had also removed part of the safety margin. And a revolver which explodes when you fire it is apt to do more damage to the marksman than to his target.

If this sort of accident had happened too often, it could account for the presence of the two young men.

The colonel lit a cigar and considered the question. The most probable answer was that they would watch him to find out what business he was engaged on in England. They would plan to put in an appearance at the precise moment when the colonel's negotiations were reaching a conclusion, and they would then threaten to make a lot of trouble with the authorities. Unless a fair share of the profits on the new deal was handed to them. Enough to compensate them for the fact that they had paid fifteen pounds each for revolvers worth, at most, five pounds.

It all depended, thought the colonel, on who had got hurt. If it had been a few unimportant officers or noncommissioned officers, money would be adequate compensation.

If, on the other hand, it had been the president's son, or one of his boyfriends, only blood would pay the bill. His blood.

The colonel moved to the window. The car which had followed him was parked on the other side of the road. One of the young men was in it. The other was out of sight.

He was about to return to his chair when the telephone rang.

He picked up the receiver and said, "Yes." And this was all

he did say for some time. When the comfortable middle-aged woman's voice at the other end had finished, he said, "Thank you so much, my dear. If you examine your bank account next week you will find that Father Christmas has not forgotten you. Let me write that address down. Number seventeen Riverside Avenue, Richmond. Lovely. Good-bye for now."

Sam Maxfeldt said, "I hope we haven't let you in for something."

"What are you talking about?" said Hugo.

"When this woman rang up I didn't think anything of it. She said she was Larry Foreman's secretary. She said Larry wanted to call on you before he left for America tomorrow and discuss a proposition. He wanted your address so I gave it to her. I shouldn't have done it, of course."

"That sounds exciting."

"But it wasn't."

"Wasn't what?"

"It wasn't Larry's secretary. When the girl told me, I thought I ought to find out more about this proposition and I rang Larry's office back. The call hadn't come from them."

"It was probably a gag by one of my fans," said Hugo. When he had become famous he had gone ex-directory, and his address was always given as Sam Maxfeldt's office.

"I expect that's it," said Sam.

At eight o'clock that same evening, Colonel Rex left Inverness Mansions. He left by the back door and walked unhurriedly to Gloucester Road underground station. He did not think he was being followed but he was taking no chances.

He caught the first train that came in. The fact that the indicator board showed that it was going to Wimbledon, and that this was almost exactly in the wrong direction, did not seem to worry him.

By the time the train had crossed the Thames and reached East Putney, he had finished his cigar, and here he got out. Without surrendering his ticket, he crossed the bridge and sat down on the deserted platform on the other side to wait for a train back to Earl's Court. This simple maneuver ensured that anyone following him would have to declare himself.

There was no one.

The colonel switched trains once more at Earl's Court and reached Richmond at ten to nine. At nine o'clock he was ringing the doorbell on Hugo's side of the house.

Hugo answered the door himself. He had been expecting a gaggle of teen-age fans, and the sight of a middle-aged man in a neat herringbone ulster, with a briefcase in one hand and a rolled umbrella in the other, took him momentarily off balance.

"Mr. Greest?"

"That's me," said Hugo. "What can I do for you?"

"I must apologize for calling at such an uncivilized hour, but I've only just landed in England."

"Well, come in," said Hugo. It seemed the only thing to say. "Let me take your coat."

He led the way up a short flight of stairs and held open the door of his sitting room. "I imagine this is something to do with Umran."

"Indeed it is," said the colonel. "But I must explain at once, in case you decide to throw me out"—he smiled as though speaking of a remote contingency—"that I have not been sent here by the Foreign Office, or by the Crown Agents."

"Then how did you—oh, I see. You're the person who rang up Sam."

"A friend of mine did it for me."

"Well," said Hugo cautiously, "now that you're here, you'd better tell me what it's all about."

"It's about arms."

"You're an arms salesman."

"Let me give you my card. My friends call me Colonel Rex. I hope you will follow suit."

"I'm afraid you're too late, Colonel. I've made all my arrangements through the Crown Agents."

"Have you signed anything?"

"Not yet."

34

"Well, thank goodness for that."

"Why?"

"I should hate to think," said the colonel, "that in the course of a single day Providence had placed a modest fortune in your hands and you had thrown it away."

"What are you talking about?"

"You are aware that there are two sources for the purchase of arms. Governments and private operators."

"Major Gilliland told me as much."

"Ah, yes. Mike Gilliland. I know him well. An excellent fellow, and good at his job. Quite the best man they have. But did he explain to you the difference between the two sources? The difference from your point of view. Perhaps not."

"Not precisely."

"And yet it's very simple. It is the only reason that private operators like myself exist. The government agencies hold all the cards. They have stocks of arms. They have technical experts at call from the armed forces. They control the necessary export licenses. But being government servants, they work within very strict financial controls. No money ends up in *their* pockets. It goes straight from the buyer—in this case the ruler of Umran—to the seller, the British Treasury."

"I suppose that's right."

"But if you buy from a private operator, the whole transaction is more in the nature of a joint venture, and the profits accrue accordingly. You, by favor of the ruler of Umran, have a potential order worth perhaps half a million pounds. I could not price it more accurately without knowing the precise details."

"You seem to have learned a good deal about it already, if I may say so."

"There is no mystery about that. The ruler of Umran was known to be over here on a shopping expedition for his new army. It is only quite recently that he has been in a position to spend big money. You know about that, of course."

"I did hear that there had been a mineral strike."

"But you don't know exactly what has been found."

"I was told, but I've forgotten."

"I see." Hugo thought that he detected, for the first time, a faint look of approval in the colonel's eyes; the look which a poker player might give an opponent whom he has assumed to be a fool when he realizes that he may have to revise his judgment.

"Let us revert to this transaction. If the sale price to Umran is half a million pounds, it should be possible, by careful selection, to buy the weapons for four hundred thousand, possibly less. There is a large element of luck in a transaction of this sort. Since the arms are for a sovereign state which is friendly to this country and is not at war with any other state, there should be no difficulty about export licenses, and therefore no need to spend money in overcoming those difficulties. The total profit should be available for distribution between the two of us. Since I should have to do most of the work, I should suggest a forty-sixty split."

"You mean," said Hugo slowly, "that if I do it through the Crown Agents I get nothing, but if I do it this way I pocket forty thousand pounds."

"An approximate figure, of course."

"Perhaps you'd care for a drink?"

Chapter 5 / Robert Ringbolt

The American eagle, embossed on the top left-hand corner of a thick sheet of ivory-white writing paper, held a bunch of arrows in one claw and an olive branch in the other. The bird was clearly keeping its options open.

The letter suggested that since Mr. Greest was about to take up a position of responsibility in the Gulf, and since important American interests existed in that area, Mr. Greest might care to discuss policy matters which might affect their respective governments. No commitment was involved, but an exchange of views might be of mutual advantage.

The letter was signed Robert Ringbolt, Third Secretary, Section of Trade and Industry.

There was a postscript in Mr. Ringbolt's own neat hand:

"I'd certainly be glad if we could meet. If it's not short notice, suggest luncheon today. Would meet you at the American Club in Piccadilly at half-past twelve. If this is impossible, could you ring the hall porter and suggest an alternative date. If no message, I'll be expecting you."

Hugo's first thought was that he ought to have a word with Mr. Taverner at the Foreign Office. His second thought was that it might be embarrassing. He was far from certain of the view that officialdom might take of his previous night's discussions with Colonel Rex.

The simplest course would be to put Mr. Ringbolt off. He would be missing a free lunch. But his experiences of American food had not always been happy. On the other hand, it might be his duty to go.

"Policy matters which might affect our respective governments."

Sir Hugo Greest, K.C.M.G. For services to the British government in the Middle East.

And after all, he had absolutely nothing else to do.

Robert Ringbolt, who was waiting for him in the foyer of the American Club, turned out to be a personable young man, as clean and sparkling as if he had just stepped out from under a television shower bath. (Commando soap, the soap that rubs virility into your pores.) His tailor had done him proud, too. He could have been the product of any public school in England or private school in America.

He came forward, walking on the balls of his feet like an athlete, presented Hugo with a firm hand grasp, and said, "No difficulty in recognizing *you*, Mr. Greest. I've seen you rescuing too many females in distress. Come along up to the bar and meet one or two people."

In the bar, which was filling up rapidly, Hugo was introduced to a number of people whose names he forgot immediately. He was then steered to a table in the corner where a middle-aged man with a brown face and crinkly gray hair was staring at a nearly empty glass. Ringbolt waved across the crowded room to a waiter. His flashing smile seemed to possess the quality of a radar signal. The waiter homed on it immediately. Three more drinks were ordered and fresh introductions were made.

This time Hugo made an effort to catch the name. He was certain that Ringbolt had said Lord Twinley. But there was a snag. Americans had, he knew, a habit of adopting Lord, Duke, and Earl as Christian names, a fact which had trapped many unwary visitors into absurdity. While his host was paying for the drinks, he said, "Did I get that right? Lord Twinley?"

"Quite right," said the man. "Bob's being very formal this morning. He usually introduces me to people as Bertie. I think he wanted to impress you."

"He's succeeded."

"Have you known Bob long?"

38

"For exactly five minutes."

"He's a good chap. Right on his toes. I imagine it's something to do with the Gulf. That's his particular interest."

"Do you know that part of the world?"

"Fairly well. I was political agent at Abu Dhabi for two years, and then I was a sort of dogsbody in the residency at Bahrain."

"Bertie," said Ringbolt, returning to the table, "is in the secret service. So don't say anything you shouldn't."

"Absolute nonsense," said Lord Twinley. "Like all Americans, Bob has got romantic notions about the British secret service. Actually, being in the racket himself, he knows perfectly well that all consular and foreign service officials are supposed to keep their eyes open and their ears flapping. If that makes me a spy, it makes him one, too."

"To espionage," said Bob. "We'll drink to that."

The martinis they were drinking must have had a lot of gin in them. After the third one, Hugo felt that his entrails were becoming anaesthetized and began to wonder about lunch.

Ringbolt appeared to read his thoughts. He said, "If you're prepared to walk a few steps, we'll be moving."

When they got out into Piccadilly, Hugo, in whom the pale spring sunlight and the gin were combining to produce a mood of euphoria, began betting with himself. The Ritz? The Caprice? No. Passed the turning. The Berkeley? Missed that one, too. What possibilities lay ahead?

"We turn left here," said Ringbolt.

Albany, by God.

The porter said, "Good afternoon, Mr. Ringbolt," and then, "Nice to see you again, Mr. Greest."

"Would he be one of your fans, too?"

"No," said Hugo. "Actually, I used to live here myself once."

"It certainly gives me a kick occupying an apartment which once belonged to Lord Byron. I expect, in years to come, they'll be putting up a plate for you, too, Hugo."

Colonel Rex had left his flat at eleven o'clock that morning. He had a number of business calls to make, and none of the business lent itself to discussion on the telephone. It all had to be done personally.

He walked down the stairs, avoiding the lift.

(He had once had a very unpleasant experience in Mexico City. The lift which was meant to take him nonstop from the twentieth to the ground floor had stopped unexpectedly at the tenth floor and a man had got in and tried to knife him. The colonel, who was an expert at knife fighting, had deflected the thrust at some cost to himself and replied in kind. When the lift arrived at the foyer and the doors opened to reveal the shambles inside, a middle-aged lady, who had been waiting for it, had had hysterics. A great many explanations had been called for.)

As he walked downstairs and out into the courtyard at the back, he was thinking about his conversation on the previous evening and trying to come to some conclusion about Hugo Greest.

Was he a fool? Or was he a crafty man who preferred to behave like a fool? Or was he a knave? Or was he possibly a simple, honest man? The colonel was experienced in dealing with the foolish, the crafty, and the dishonest. It was the final category that he found disconcerting. Their reactions were difficult to anticipate. They followed no predictable course.

He came out into the courtyard and sniffed the morning air with approval. It was a day of premature spring weather. The colonel had never been able to understand why the English complained about their weather. It was variable, but almost entirely temperate and agreeable.

He unlocked the garage door and the door of his car. As he was about to get in, he checked. It was such a brief pause, a tiny cessation of movement, that a watcher would hardly have detected it. At one moment he was getting into his car. At the next, he was leaning over the back of the driving seat, picking up the light overcoat from the back seat.

Then he backed out of the car, shut the door very gently, and locked it. He locked up the garage again, pocketed the keys, and put on the overcoat. It was such a nice day 'that he had evidently decided to walk or use public transport.

A sensible decision, one might have felt, in view of the congested streets of central London and the near impossibility of parking.

"So that's the position," said Ringbolt. "Bertie will tell you if I'm painting with too broad a brush."

An extremely pleasant luncheon, served by a middle-aged housekeeper, had been followed by coffee and brandy. Hugo lit the cigar which was offered to him and tried to keep his defensive mechanisms in trim. It was not easy.

Whether Lord Twinley was in the secret service or not, he had certainly been in the Gulf, and he knew what he was talking about. Bob seemed to have done his homework, too.

"When you decided to withdraw from the Gulf—" he said, "and I'm not criticizing the decision; it was pretty inevitable, I guess—you left a vacuum. And nature, as I was taught at school, abhors a vacuum. Moreover, there was no shortage of people waiting to fill it. The United States has got more money invested in those parts than they'd care to see threatened. Our main ally is Saudi Arabia. The Russians are pressing down on Iran. They're pretty unwilling partners in some ways, but a competitive situation makes strange bedfellows, and I happen to know that Kedried, their minister for oil and fuel, has been in Teheran these last few months. And last, but by no means least "—Ringbolt tapped off the ash of his cigar with a composed gesture which suddenly made Hugo realize that he was a lot older than he looked— "last but not least, the Chinese are moving north from their first outpost, Aden, and getting their feet under the table in Iraq. The Ba'ath party are just natural colleagues for them. The smaller states line up with the bigger ones. Bahrain with Saudi, Qatar with Iran, and so on."

"And Umran."

"If I was a cartoonist," said Lord Twinley, "I'd draw the whole thing for you in a picture. Tiny little Umran, wearing a miniskirt and a bashful smile. Three enormous suitors, pressing forward to demand her hand in marriage. Each of them with a bunch of flowers in one fist and a submachine gun in the other."

Hugo said, "That hardly fits in with my impression of Sheik

Ahmed bin Rashid bin Abdullah al Ferini. I don't see him in a miniskirt somehow."

"He's quite a boy," said Ringbolt. "But he's still only got half a division of troops."

"His idea seems to be that a small army that's prepared to fight is better than a large one sitting on a pile of atomic weapons it daren't use."

"Something in that," said Lord Twinley. "And he's certainly got them at the spot where it counts. Have you ever worked out what would happen if someone did blockade the mouth of the Gulf? Suez would be peanuts to it. The oil companies got round that one by building big tankers and routing their oil round the Cape. There's no alternative route out of the Gulf. Except by pipe line across the desert. Which could be blown up half a dozen times a week."

It was at this moment that the telephone rang. Ringbolt lifted the receiver, listened for a moment, and said, "It's for you, Hugo."

"Can't be," said Hugo. "Who is it?"

"Mrs. Greest, she said."

It was his mother. She said, "I'm so sorry to chase you like this, darling. But I rang up that American Club and they gave me this number. They were terribly sticky about it, but when I told them how urgent it was—"

"What's happened?"

"It's this terrible American. I can't make him go away."

"What American?"

"He said Mr. Ringbolt—"

"I'm with Mr. Ringbolt now."

"No, no. He isn't Mr. Ringbolt. He mentioned Mr. Ringbolt's name, and I knew you were having lunch with him, so I let him in. Now I can't get rid of him. Hugo, you've got to come back and cope."

When his mother spoke in that tone of voice, the discipline of the nursery reasserted itself. He said, "All right. I'll be back."

When he got back to Richmond he went straight in by the front door on his mother's side of the house. His mother was waiting in the hall. She said, in a whisper, "I couldn't sit there just looking at him. In the end I *had* to come out. Do get rid of him."

"Who is he?"

"He gave me this."

The card, which was twice the size of an ordinary visiting card, said, "Urban L. Nussbaum," in large letters, and in smaller letters in the bottom right-hand corner, "Suite 1005, Grand Central Building, Topeka, Kansas, U.S.A."

"All right," said Hugo. "I'll deal with him."

He strode into the drawing room and Mr. Nussbaum rose to greet him. Rose was the appropriate word. He came imperceptibly upward, like a balloon from its moorings. He was such an odd shape that Hugo got the impression that he was smaller when standing up than when sitting down. His bulk was encased in a gray suit and he was wearing a tie which put Sayyed Nawaf's in the shade.

His face, nut brown shading to gray black round the jowls, broke into a warm smile at the sight of Hugo.

"I certainly am glad to meet you, Mr. Greest."

"I can't say the same until I know what it's all about."

"Of course, of course."

"And I don't usually talk business in my mother's drawing room."

"Naturally not, and I wouldn't have intruded if I hadn't assumed this was all your residence. I had no idea that part of it belonged to your mother. A fine old lady. I hope she soon recovers."

"Recovers?"

"I detected that she was not quite herself. She informed me that she was suffering from a migraine."

"It comes and goes," said Hugo. "Suppose we move to my side of the house." He led the way up the stairs, through a door, and into his quarters. "You are from Target, I take it?"

Mr. Nussbaum's eyes twinkled in the depths of his cheeks. He said, "I must congratulate you on your intelligence system. You know of our little organization."

"I heard the name for the first time yesterday. I'm afraid you're too late."

"I'm never too late," said Mr. Nussbaum genially. "If I miss one train, I catch the next. If I miss that one, I hire a special. You haven't signed any papers, I hope."

Hugo admitted that he had not signed anything. It was apparently a mistake in the arms business to sign papers.

"In that case, I'm not too late. Any offer Abacus made you, I can cut five percent off it. Maybe ten."

"Not Abacus. A gentleman called Colonel Leroy Delmaison."

Insofar as it was possible to read any expression in the involuted surface of his visitor's face, Hugo thought he detected the beginnings of a thoughtful look. It was as though a cloud had passed across an upland valley, removing the warmth, bringing with it a hint of snow.

"The gentleman you have mentioned is a very able operator. Right on the mark, too. But you have to appreciate, Mr. Greest, that he is only a middleman. He has no sources of supply himself."

"He seemed to think that he would be able to organize them. We had a long talk last night."

"Colonel Rex can certainly talk. But talk won't produce articles he hasn't got. Did he mention antiaircraft guns? Or medium guns on mobile mountings?"

"Not specifically, no."

"Did he think to tell you that these particular items were only obtainable from one firm in Sweden? And that Target had exclusive distribution rights in all the products of that firm?"

"No," said Hugo slowly. "No, he didn't tell me that. Is it a fact?"

"Why should I lie to you, when you can check on it so easily? You can ask him yourself."

"I could do that."

"Now, I'm not saying anything against Colonel Rex, you understand. He's a smart operator. He's entitled to make you a proposition. I'm entitled to make you a proposition. You select the one that suits you best. Right?"

44

"The only thing is, I did give him a sort of option—"

"Not in writing?"

"No, not in writing. But I don't like going back on my word."

"It does you credit," said Mr. Nussbaum heartily. "Here's an idea to play around with. Why don't you do business with *both* of us?"

Colonel Rex was turning into Riverside Avenue, Richmond, when he stopped. Parked opposite number 17 was a red American sedan. It was a distinctive sort of car. Not only was it twice as long as the average English car, but it seemed to bulge in unexpected places. The colonel examined it with interest for some seconds, and then walked back the way he had come, retired up a side turning, and settled down to wait.

When Hugo woke next morning, the weather had broken. The first days of false spring had flattered to deceive. The pale sunlight was gone. The winds of March were blowing bleakly and they had brought rain with them.

"What an extraordinary man!" said his mother.

Hugo, as was his habit when he was not working, had walked down to spend the half hour after breakfast with her.

"I'm sorry you got lumbered with him."

"It was an experience. He wasn't offensive, you know. Quite the contrary. He was very polite. But it all went on rather long."

"Did you notice his tie?"

"It was very striking. He told me about it. It was based on a painting by Picasso. He told me about everything. It was like the Poles during the war. Of course, you were too young to remember them. *They* told you about everything, too. The most terrible things had happened to all of them."

"I hope Mr. Nussbaum didn't tell you anything terrible."

"On the contrary. He seems to have had a very happy life. Both his children are at a university. Can you imagine?"

"In America everyone goes to university."

"He started in the army in the ranks and rose to be a master sergeant gunner. Or it might have been sergeant master gunner. Then, after the war, he sold vacuum cleaners for a bit, and then he started selling other things."

"Did he tell you what things?"

"I think he said something about guns."

"That's right."

46

"He's a gun runner?"

"They're more politely described as arms dealers."

"How very interesting."

Hugo had noticed before that things which ought to shock or upset his mother hardly worried her at all. It was the minor irritations and stupidities of life which infuriated her. People who drove their cars too fast or too close to the pavement on wet days, or signed their names to multiple letters in the *Times*.

She said, "You mustn't tell me about it, of course, if it's confidential."

"I don't see why I shouldn't," said Hugo.

His mother listened to him, with her head slightly on one side in a birdlike attitude. It was from her that Hugo had inherited his artistic flair, rather than from his father, a large, silent man, who had been killed by the Japanese at Imphal.

She said, "Do I gather that the choice is between buying all these things from the government or buying them from a private firm?"

"That's more or less what it amounts to."

"Well, I know which I'd choose."

"The government."

"Certainly not. Civil servants have no business morality at all."

"Businessmen don't seem to have much morality either."

"No. But they have some. Even if it's only based on self-protection. They don't swindle other businessmen, because the people they've swindled might get their own back. But a government doesn't mind about that. It's so big it thinks no one can hurt it. It's like doing business with a boa constrictor."

"You sound as though you have been dickering with government departments all your life."

"I had a good deal to do with them when your father was killed. I remember when I tried to get some money out of them to send you away to school. They were totally unhelpful. I can still see that silly little man, saying to me, 'The state provides a perfectly adequate education, Mrs. Greest.' I just picked up the inkpot on his desk and threw it at him."

"I don't suppose that made him any more helpful."

Mrs. Greest gave a throaty chuckle and said, "It made *me* feel a lot better. And what happened? That very same day your uncle came along and told me he'd got a nomination to Christ's Hospital. They were marvelous. Give me private enterprise every time."

At ten o'clock that morning, Colonel Rex telephoned the hotel at which he had discovered that Mr. Nussbaum was staying, and was told that he had gone out but would be back within the hour.

At eleven o'clock he telephoned again. Mr. Nussbaum had returned and was somewhere in the hotel. Would he like to have him paged?

The colonel said no. He did not think that this would be advisable. But perhaps reception would give him a telephone number to ring back. Reception said it could do this.

At twelve o'clock Mr. Nussbaum telephoned the colonel. Mutual courtesies were exchanged, mutual friends remembered, inquiries made about each other's families. Mrs. Nussbaum was in excellent health. The colonel's old father was still alive. A wonderful man for his age.

Protocol having been observed, Mr. Nussbaum suggested that it might be to both their advantages if they had a little talk. The colonel thought that this might be a good idea. But when, and where?

"I don't think," said Mr. Nussbaum, "that it would be a very good idea if we were seen talking together. You know how tongues wag in our line of business."

"They certainly do," said the colonel. "I'll tell you what. I've got a quiet little flat here. Why don't you come over? I'd suggest about eight o'clock this evening. We could have a drink and talk things over."

"Seems like a good idea," said Mr. Nussbaum.

"After that, maybe we could go together and put a proposition to our mutual client."

"Our mutual client?" said Mr. Nussbaum cautiously.

"I was referring to a Mr. Greest, who resides at number

seventeen Riverside Avenue, Richmond. I believe you spent some time with him yesterday. He will have told you that I saw him the day before."

There was short pause, and then Mr. Nussbaum said, in a much more businesslike voice, "O.K. We're in this together. We'll have to work out the split. Right?"

"Right. And as soon as we've worked it out, we put it to Mr. Greest and sign him up, before anyone else gets ideas about coming in on the act. Right?"

"The sooner the better."

"I had an open date to go along and talk to him after dinner tonight. We might go along together. I suggest—" At this point, anyone observing the colonel would have noticed a curious repetition of what had taken place the day before, when he opened the door of his car. On that occasion he had started to do one thing and it had changed, easily and almost imperceptibly, into something else. This time the same thing happened to what he was saying. "I suggest," he said, and there was the barest pause after the word, "that I run us both up in my car. It's one I hired when I came over. There's nothing to connect it with me."

"Fine," said Mr. Nussbaum.

Hugo thought that it would be easier if he dealt with Major Gilliland on the telephone. He rang him up and recognized the voice of his secretary. She said that the major was on another line, and would he mind holding? Hugo said he didn't mind at all. In fact, it gave him time to think out exactly what he was going to say.

When the major's dry voice said, "Mr. Greest. You wanted me?" Hugo was ready. He said, "You very kindly offered to introduce me to your Ordnance people. The idea being that they could improve any nonexistent technical knowledge. I wonder if you'd put it off for a bit."

"I haven't fixed anything yet."

"Oh, good."

"Has there been a change of plan, then?"

"In a way. I'm taking on an adviser. A man who seems to know about these things. I thought I ought to listen, first, to what he has to tell me before making my mind up."

"Quite right. Don't hesitate to come back here if you think we can help."

"I'll do that," said Hugo, and rang off. It had been easier than he had expected.

Major Gilliland replaced the receiver at his end and said to his secretary, "I'm afraid someone's got in ahead of us. Pity."

"They certainly keep their ears to the ground," said his secretary.

Mr. Nussbaum was not sorry that Colonel Rex had suggested eight o'clock that evening for their meeting. He had much to do. First he had to compose a long and complicated telex message. This could go direct from the hotel, which he had chosen for its telex facilities, to his headquarters in Topeka. There would be time for an answer to reach him before he set out for his rendezvous.

After attending to this, he had his second shave of the day and a facial massage in the barbershop attached to the hotel, and took a cup of tea in the lounge. Despite his size and shape, he was not a gross eater. He drank alcohol solely in the line of business. When he was by himself, he preferred soft drinks.

At five o'clock, the answer to his telex arrived. He took it up to his room and decoded it, making pencil notes in the margin. Then he locked it away in his briefcase, which had a combination lock set to the date of his wife's birthday.

After this he took out his address book and made a number of telephone calls. The three men he called were in their offices. They all seemed to be late workers. The last call was concluded at a quarter past seven.

He then washed his hands, scrubbing his nails carefully as if to remove the grime of the day's work, belted on a raincoat, put on a pair of pigskin gloves, and took the lift down to the ground floor.

He stopped at the reception desk to say, "I shan't be back

50

until quite late. If anyone wants me, suggest they call again tomorrow morning, would you?"

The receptionist, who knew Mr. Nussbaum as a big tipper, said he would certainly do that. It then occurred to Mr. Nussbaum that if, as usually seemed to happen, the arrival of the rain had meant the departure of all available taxis, he had little idea of how to get to Inverness Mansions.

The receptionist suggested that a District Line or Circle Line train would take him to Gloucester Road station, from which it would not be more than five minutes' walk. Mr. Nussbaum thanked him, turned up the collar of his raincoat, and stepped out, briefcase in hand. He was looking forward to the bargaining match, the contest of bluff and skill, the game of commercial poker which he foresaw.

As he arrived at Inverness Mansions, a policeman was coming out. There was a police car drawn up at the curb. In the foyer, the hall porter was talking to a worried-looking little man in pin-stripe trousers and a black coat, whom Mr. Nussbaum assumed to be the manager. It took some time to attract their attention.

When he asked for number 28, they both looked at him sharply, and the manager said, "Would you be the doctor?"

"No," said Mr. Nussbaum. "Just a business acquaintance. I had an appointment with him at eight."

"I think a doctor ought to see him first."

"He was quite definite, Mr. Parrock, that he did *not* require a doctor. Quite definite, he was."

"What's happened?" said Mr. Nussbaum.

"He was attacked," said the porter. "Two men. Foreigners, he says. As he was coming in through the back door."

"The police have the matter in hand," said the manager.

"Was he badly hurt?"

"It seems he got a cut on the right hand. And wrenched his left shoulder. In my opinion, he should have seen a doctor at once."

"I know Colonel Delmaison fairly well," said Mr. Nussbaum. "He has had what you might call an adventurous career. A

51

matter which might seem to you and me to call for medical attention may appear in a different light to him."

"Ah, well," said the manager, "that puts a rather different complexion on it. The flat's on the second floor. If he should want anything, tell him to ring down. The sergeant will look after it."

When Mr. Nussbaum pressed the bell of flat 28, there was a short pause. Then a shuffle of footsteps and a further pause, and the colonel's voice: "Who is it?"

"Nussbaum here."

"All right. Hold on while I operate this bloody handle."

When the door was opened, Mr. Nussbaum appreciated his host's difficulty. His left arm was in a sling and his right hand was heavily bandaged.

"Come in," said the colonel. "Shut the door. Pour yourself out a drink. The Scotch is in the corner cupboard. You can give me one, too. Don't be stingy with it."

"What on earth happened?"

"What happened," said the colonel morosely, "was that I was jumped. At my age, too. I'd put the car away. They must have been waiting for me just inside the back door. Thanks."

He held the glass between the fingers of his padded right hand and tipped some whisky down his throat. Mr. Nussbaum noticed that some blood had soaked through the bandages.

"Shouldn't you have that looked after properly?" he said.

"Just a scratch. The porter tied it up for me. He's an old soldier. Made a good job of it."

"How did you . . . ?"

"Got it when I grabbed the knife. I had to move quickly. The other one was coming for me."

"What did you do?"

"I kicked him in the goolies," said the colonel. "That taught him the time of day. Luckily that porter came along, and they scarpered. He helped me up here and patched me up."

"We'd better call off our visit tonight."

"Call off nothing," said the colonel. "Do you think I'm going to sidetrack business for a scratch on the hand and a wrenched shoulder. I remember once in Bolivia when General Martínez gave me a bucko horse to ride. The old devil did it on purpose. It threw me off and I broke my right arm. I signed the contract before I'd see a doctor. It's the only one I've signed left-handed."

Mr. Nussbaum, who had heard this story before, and disbelieved it, said, "We shan't get a taxi. I can promise you that."

"We'll use my car."

"You can't drive it."

"No, but you can. Feel in my inside pocket. You'll find the keys. The Yale is the garage door. The small one with a number on it is the car key. It's an Austin 1800. Right-hand drive. Apart from that, everything in the normal positions. O.K.?"

"O.K.," said Mr. Nussbaum. "I'll bring her around to the front." At the door, he paused and looked back at the colonel, who was finishing his drink, the glass held awkwardly in his padded right hand.

"You're a tough old devil, aren't you?" he said, with an unwilling note of admiration in his voice.

After he had gone, Colonel Rex remained standing, perfectly still. Then he said to himself, "I'm a tough old devil." It was as though he was reassuring himself about something.

Then came the roar of the explosion.

Even two stories up, the blast was powerful enough to crack the window glass. The curtains billowed gently inward.

Chapter 7 / Arms and Money

"Did you arrange to have him blown up, Mr. Greest?"

"No, Hussein. I did not."

"Excuse the remark," said Sheik Ahmed. "The boy forgets his manners."

"But in one of the Tiger stories," said Prince Hussein, "—it was called 'The Tiger Strikes Back.' It took place in Algeria—"

"If you cannot talk sensibly," said his father, "I shall have to order you to leave the room. Apologize at once."

"I'm sorry," said Prince Hussein. But he did not sound sorry. Hugo had the impression that in some way the happenings of the previous evening had raised his stock in the eyes of the heir to the throne of Umran.

"We saw a report in the papers," said the ruler. "Have you any idea what occurred?"

"Colonel Rex telephoned me this morning. There were two men. Haitians or Dominicans, he thought. Foreigners certainly. They had made one attempt to kill him already that evening. The colonel escaped with a wrenched shoulder and a cut hand."

"What did he do to them?" said Hussein.

"He didn't tell me."

"Perhaps he had a knife himself."

"Let Mr. Greest continue with his story."

"The police were called. They took a statement and promised to have one of their men keep an eye on the block. While they were doing this, the two men must have slipped out at the back and put an explosive charge in the colonel's car. It was garaged at the back."

54

"The car would be locked. The garage, too, perhaps. How would they get in?"

"That's a mystery. And likely to remain one. There is very little left of the car or the garage, you understand."

"And it was the other man, the American, who went down to fetch the car because the colonel was disabled?"

"That's right."

"And was blown up instead of him?"

"It would seem so."

"Will the men be caught?"

"Probably. The policeman on duty gave the alarm at once. The airports were all warned. The ports, too."

"Could they have reached the airport *before* the warning?"

"The police think not. Between the assault and the explosion was less than an hour. And much of that must have been spent in fixing the explosive. They could hardly have done all that *and* reached the airport."

The ruler considered the matter, stroking his head thoughtfully. He said, "Providence moves in a mysterious way. Three attempts have been made to kill me. One was prevented by the diligence of my guards. The other two by simple chance. On one occasion because I was late for an appointment. On another because I was sitting in the front of the car, not the back. These matters are doubtless ordained."

The ruler appeared to dismiss the matter from his thoughts. He turned to Sayyed Nawaf, who had been sitting quietly in the background, and said, "Will you explain to Mr. Greest the arrangements we have made for money to be available."

Sayyed Nawaf opened his briefcase. Hugo thought, for a moment, that he was going to produce an enormous bundle of currency. What came out were two documents. Nawaf said, "We have opened letters of credit, Mr. Greest. One with the National Westminster Bank at its head office in London for one hundred twenty thousand pounds. A second one at the head office of the Arab Bank in Beirut for four hundred eighty thousand pounds. These are copies of the documents. We understand that it is customary, in purchasing arms, to put down a deposit of not more than twenty percent. Credits of up to

shall have to go shopping in Belgium. That being so, I'd like to get everything else there except the ammunition. We're up against some fairly tight time limits."

He looked at Nawaf, who so far had said nothing. He continued to say nothing.

"You won't buy tracked vehicles in Belgium," said the CSO. "What you need are light Weasels or Snowcats. What'll go across snow will go across sand."

The colonel drew a loop on the paper in front of him, then another loop, and joined them together by a line. Then he said, "All right, we'll buy them in Milan, have them railed to Bari, and pick them up on our way out. I'd like to pick up the Spanish ammunition, too, but we can't chance two stops. A modern boat, which doesn't waste time, should make Beirut in twelve days with one stop at Bari. But it doesn't leave much margin. I suppose there's no chance of stretching these dates, Sayyed?"

Nawaf said, "It is essential that the arms be with us by the end of April. It is for that reason that His Highness has instructed me to draw the letters of credit with strict time clauses."

Hugo said, "Would someone please explain. I thought letters of credit were the same as cash."

"Cash with a time fuse," said the colonel. "This London letter is worth one hundred twenty thousand pounds to us, *if* it is presented to the bank before close of business on April fifteenth. One minute later it is worth nothing."

"Then let's present it right away."

"Before the bank will pay out on it, they will need to see invoices covering all the goods purchased, bills of lading showing that they are on ship at London Docks, and a certificate from the government inspectors here that they have examined all items and found them to be in good workmanlike condition."

Hugo said, "Oh, I see. I'd no idea it was so complicated. Are we going to be able to do all that in time?"

"It's now March twenty-fifth."

"So it is. Lady Day."

Nawaf, who had been following these exchanges with interest, said, "You have a special day set aside for ladies?"

58

"I don't think it means that exactly. It's one of our old quarter days. I think it's got a religious significance."

"It's got this significance for us," said the colonel. "That we've got exactly three weeks to do a hell of a lot of work in. We've got to have all this stuff except the tracked vehicles examined here. Since they're new, I take it you'll accept factory certificates?"

Nawaf nodded.

"Before we can bring the guns in from Belgium, we'll need an import license."

"No difficulty there," said the CSO.

"Agreed. And an export permit to get it all out of this country. That's sometimes more difficult. How often does the committee meet?"

"Once a week," said the CSO. "There'll be no difficulty about an export permit if you can produce an end-use certificate."

"Sayyed Nawaf should be able to do that for us."

Nawaf said, "Please explain." Hugo felt pleased that someone else was out of his depth.

"It's a certificate from the ruler that all these arms are for use in his own territory of Umran and not for export."

Nawaf smiled faintly and said, "There will be no difficulty about that. You shall have it at once. Does that solve your difficulties? Can you conform to the required dates?"

"It solves one difficulty," said Colonel Rex. "The others we shall see as and when they arise. I've never known a transaction of this sort to go through absolutely smoothly from beginning to end."

When Hugo got home, he found a note on his hall table from his mother. It said, "A policeman called to see you." And underneath, "He called again. I said you'd telephone him when you got home. Dial 2323. Ask for Inspector Hayman."

Hugo dialed the number and was told that Inspector Hayman was out, but would be given a message as soon as he got back. This was a nuisance, as he had planned to go out himself. Instead he went down to talk to his mother, carrying a bottle of sherry with him.

"You know I never ask questions about your work," said his mother, "but what on earth have you been up to? First that terrible American, and then the police—twice."

"That terrible American," said Hugo, "is dead. It was in the papers this morning."

His mother said, "Good heavens!" and took a large gulp of her sherry. "Heart failure, I suppose. He didn't look very healthy."

"Heart failure would be one way of describing it." He found the paragraph in the *Daily Telegraph* and showed it to her. His mother read it through, her lips compressed into a tight line. She then examined the photograph of what was left of the garage and the car, and said, "So it was all a mistake. Not that that's much consolation to his poor little wife."

"None at all."

"Do you suppose that's what the police want to talk to you about?"

"I expect it is," said Hugo. "And this looks like them." Headlights showed at the gate, a car door slammed, and a man got out. He said, "I'll take him round my side."

Detective Inspector Hayman turned out to have longish pale hair and a pale mustache, and to smoke a cigarette in a pale amber cigarette holder. He said, "I expect you can guess what this is all about, Mr. Greest. The American gentleman who got himself blown up down in Kensington. I understand he came up to see you, is that right? Sometime on Thursday evening. Could you tell us what it was all about?"

Hugo told him. The inspector listened with a faint smile on his face and said, "Cloak and dagger stuff, eh?"

"Not really. Straightforward buying and selling. All aboveboard and subject to license."

"I hope so," said the Inspector. "I've heard it's a rough business. This other man, the French Canadian. Had he been to see you?"

"He was here on the Wednesday evening."

"And they were competing for the job?"

60

"It started that way. But as I understood it, they were cooperating, not competing. Colonel Delmaison was able to supply some of the stuff. Mr. Nussbaum was going to get hold of the rest, through his contacts in Sweden. It was to have been a partnership."

" 'Merchants of Death,' " said the inspector.

"I suppose you could call them that."

"No, no. That was the title of one of your episodes. 'Merchants of Death.' We always watch them. My children wouldn't miss them for the world. I remember it particularly. It was the one about the Bulgarian scientist. He'd invented a deadly form of nerve gas, which he was planning to sell to the Chinese. You blew him up in his own laboratory."

"So I did," said Hugo. "I'd quite forgotten."

"Rather a coincidence, wasn't it?"

Chapter 8 / Tammy

On Monday, after breakfast, Hugo's telephone rang. A female voice told him to hold the line, and Raymond Taverner came on.

He said, "I thought you ought to know that Sheik Ahmed flew back to Umran last night."

"I didn't know," said Hugo.

"He asked me to apologize for him. He tried to get hold of you but wasn't able to. He had to go in rather a hurry. As a matter of fact, we were lucky to get air passage for the whole party at such short notice."

"Why did he have to go? Has something happened?"

"There's always something happening in a place like Umran," said Taverner cautiously. "I gathered from our contact man out there—his name's Martin Cowcroft, by the way; I should make a note of it. He might be useful to you."

Hugo scribbled "Martin Cowcroft" in the blank space beside the *Times* crossword and said, "Yes. Please go on."

"It's younger brother trouble. That sort of thing's endemic in Arab sheikdoms. Son number two can never see why son number one should get all the berries."

"What *sort* of trouble?"

"Mobs out making a nuisance of themselves. Public disorder. The sooner you're out there to keep an eye on things the better, I should think."

"I can't go till I'm sent for," said Hugo. "The ruler seems to think that if I stay in London, I can do something to hurry those arms along."

"I expect he needs the arms, too," said Taverner. "If only to maintain order among his faithful subjects. Well, we'd better keep in touch."

Keeping in touch, thought Hugo. Everything seemed to turn on keeping in touch. Sit beside your telephone. Don't go out. If you do, someone will be sure to ring up. Colonel Rex was a dedicated telephoner. Long conversations would take place in which the colonel did all the talking and Hugo did all the listening. All he had been asked to contribute so far, apart from being an audience, was his signature to about a hundred documents. These he was able to sign under a power of attorney which he held from Sayyed Nawaf.

When a signing session was called for, it usually took place in Sam Maxfeldt's office. Colonel Rex was no longer at Inverness Mansions. Apparently the destruction of their garage and the loss of most of the glass on one side, coupled with the attentions of the police, had been too much for the nerves of the management and the colonel had been invited to leave. He had had two different addresses since then.

It was toward the end of the first week in April that the summons came. Sam telephoned him in the early evening and said, "Your Canadian boyfriend wants a session with you."

"At your office?"

"Not this time."

"Why not?"

"He's got an idea this place is being watched. He says he's seen some odd characters hanging about. I told him that Covent Garden was permanently full of odd characters, but he wasn't convinced. He wants you to go to the Clydesmuir Hotel."

"Where on earth is that?"

"It's in a street off Little Russell."

Hugo located the Clydesmuir Hotel and was shown up to the colonel's room by an elderly lady in black with a nose that nearly touched her chin. The room had not been designed for business conferences, and contained not much more than a bed, a dressing table, and a single chair. The air was heavy with cigar smoke, a fact which made the old lady sniff reprovingly.

"Sit on the bed," said the colonel as soon as the door was shut. "We're up against it."

"How do you mean?"

"It's those bloody Target people. I knew they'd blame Nussbaum's accident on me. They're moving heaven and earth to block our purchases. There's not a lot they can do in this country, but they've got local agents in Belgium and Spain and they're busy spreading a buzz that we're not good for the money."

"But that's nonsense."

"Of course it is. But the difficulty is that we can't cash our first letter of credit until the stuff's on ship at London Docks. Then we can pay the deposit. The English suppliers will accept that. They can have the ship stopped if the money isn't forthcoming. The Italians could do the same when she calls at Bari. The Belgians and Spaniards aren't so happy. They've got to let the stuff go out of the country on a promise."

"How much is involved?"

"The artillery is the big item. It accounts for nearly a third of the deposit."

Hugo thought about it. He said, "Then we need forty thousand pounds cash on loan for a few days."

"Right. Have you got it?"

"Certainly not. I thought you might have."

"Think again," said the colonel, and lit a fresh cigar. For some seconds the two men stared at each other across the drifting clouds of smoke. "Have a drink. It may help you to think."

It might have been the drink, or it might have been the desire to get out of the room before he was asphyxiated, but Hugo found and put forward a possible solution quite quickly.

The colonel listened to it carefully and said, "It might work. Only for God's sake don't waste any time. We want that money right away."

"I'm surely glad to see you," said Robert Ringbolt. "Let Tammy here take your overcoat. Sit yourself right down."

The girl referred to as Tammy had been the first thing Hugo

64

had noticed on coming into the office. His profession had made him a connoisseur of girls. This was one for the book. She had a trim but very clearly feminine figure, well-shaped legs which she was not ashamed to show up to the Plimsoll line and even a fraction above, and red-gold hair which was cut short and fitted her head like a copper-colored biretta, giving her at first sight a boyish look which was contradicted by her eyes and by the generous lips behind which, open in a half smile, there showed a row of sharp little teeth. Her nose was not snub but short, and her skin was pale, with the few freckles or sun spots that often went with that hair color.

Take each separate ingredient, thought Hugo, mix together, simmer in a moderate oven and serve up hot, and you had every American boy's ideal dish.

He handed her his coat absent-mindedly. Human nature being the incomplete thing it is, there must be liabilities to go with all those lovely assets. What could they be? Unpleasant voice? Stupidity? Coldness?

He was rewarded for his coat with a warm smile. He immediately switched on the stuffy English upper-class look which had enraged ninety-one different villains. The girl said, just above her breath, "Catch that Tiger."

"Tammy," said Ringbolt. "Try to behave like a secretary, even if you can't type."

"Yes, sir," said Tammy. And at the door, "I can type, too."

"Sit down," said Ringbolt with a sigh. "And tell me what brings you along this fine morning. Not that I'm not glad to see you anyway."

"I'm not sure that you're going to be when you hear what I want."

"As long as you don't want Tammy."

"I'm not aiming as high as that," said Hugo. "All I need is a loan of forty thousand pounds for about ten days."

"That's, say, a hundred thousand dollars, right?"

"It sounds more when you put it that way."

"And seeing you've come to see me, Hugo, I guess that means you want the loan from Uncle Sam."

65

"Not from you personally, certainly."

"I'm glad about that. Well, now, let's chew it over. It's not going to be easy. Uncle Sam's become something of a tightwad lately. A few years ago, he'd have said yes before you'd finished asking. In fact, there was a time, just after the war, which we're both too young to remember, when he went around Europe, Africa, and Asia with his wallet wide open trying to dish out greenbacks to people who were too damned tired to stoop down and pick them up. Things are a bit different now."

It occurred to Hugo that Ringbolt was talking to give himself time to think. Anyway, he hadn't said no yet.

"When I put it to my masters, the first thing they're going to say to me is, what sort of security can you offer?"

"I can deposit with you a letter of credit for one hundred twenty thousand pounds on a London bank."

"If you've got all that money on tap, why would you need forty thousand pounds?"

Hugo explained why he needed forty thousand pounds. Ringbolt said, "So what we're betting on is that your Colonel Rex produces all the shooting irons, in good working order, at London Docks by April fifteenth. That's in ten days' time. If he does, you get your money and you can pay us back. If he doesn't, we get nothing. I'm not being unfriendly, Hugo, I'm just trying to sort out the facts."

"That's not quite true," said Hugo. "Because at that point we'd have got the heavy stuff over from Belgium and the ammunition from Spain, and paid a cash deposit on both consignments. We'd be prepared to give you a bill of sale on all that stuff. I don't know about the guns, but you could probably sell the .308 ammunition in this country at a profit. I'm told it's in short supply."

"It sounds better than when you started. There's just one more question. I know you won't mind me asking it. O.K., we could do this. There's a bit of a risk in it. Not a lot, perhaps, if the deal's set up properly. But if we did it, it'd be a favor. What do we get back in exchange?"

Hugo had noticed before that when Americans talked busi-

66

ness they abandoned, without embarrassment, all their preliminary banalities and came to the point with refreshing brutality.

He said, picking his words carefully, "What you get, Bob, is my help and cooperation."

"That could be worth quite a bit. I won't conceal from you the fact that my masters are becoming more than a little interested in Umran. If the rest of the smitherite trial drillings assay as well as the first samples, we could be very interested indeed. But you'd know more about that than I do."

"Not much more," said Hugo cautiously. He remembered now that smitherite was the mineral that had been mentioned before. By Taverner or by the ruler? Certainly he had heard it. He mustn't forget it again.

Ringbolt said, "We'll have an opportunity to look into it when we meet out there."

"Out in Umran?"

"I told you we were interested. Interested enough to send out a small trade mission. I've been nominated to head it."

"That's good news."

"Good news for both of us. I gather that Umran's a lively little place at this precise moment. You've heard the reports?"

"The Foreign Office told me there'd been some trouble. They thought it was being stirred up by the ruler's brother."

"Sheik Hammuz. Quite a character."

"You must know that the ruler flew back ten days ago to attend to it."

"And he certainly has attended to it. There was some trouble the day after he got there. Something halfway between a large deputation and a small mob. The ruler personally gave the orders to have it dispersed. His personal police force did the rest."

"Were there a lot of casualties?"

"There's nothing like a reliable report available yet. The first count was ten killed and thirty wounded."

"Ten *killed?*"

"They don't use water cannon and rubber bullets to disperse a mob in Umran."

67

"Evidently not," said Hugo, trying to keep the shock out of his voice. "I won't keep you any longer. Will you be able to let me know soon?"

"I'll give you the answer tomorrow," said Ringbolt. "Stay by your telephone around ten o'clock. If I was a betting man, I'd say you had an odds-on chance of pulling this off."

When Hugo recovered his coat from Tammy, he gave her a smile and was answered by a lightning performance, in dumb show, of a nice girl to whom an improper suggestion has been made.

He hoped she was coming out to Umran with the trade mission. Whatever her faults might turn out to be, they were unlikely to include dullness.

Later, he telephoned Colonel Rex's hotel, to give him the encouraging news. The aged retainer, when she had finally grasped who he was and what he wanted, said that Mr. Dell Mason had left the hotel the previous evening.

"Did he leave a forwarding address?"

The aged retainer said yes, he had left an address. She'd written it down, and if he'd hang on she'd get it for him. He hung on for a very long time indeed, and had almost given up hope when a gasping and wheezing heralded her return. As she spelled out Colonel Rex's new address for him, word by word, he realized that it was Sam Maxfeldt's office.

He thanked her politely and rang off.

The colonel came through at nine o'clock the next morning. Hugo said, "You might have warned me that you were going to do another of your moonlight flits."

"I didn't know myself until it happened."

"What happened?"

"Nothing happened. But it might have. The hotel was being watched."

"Who by?"

"If I knew that, I'd be a lot happier about it."

"Where are you stopping now?"

"I won't mention it on the telephone if you don't mind. I'm speaking from a call box."

"When Hugo started to tell him about his talk with Ringbolt, the colonel cut him short. "I've been onto Bob already," he said. "The money's promised. You did a good job there, Hugo."

"Thank you."

"The best plan will be for me to ring you every day at about this time. If we have to meet, we'll make it the usual place."

"You mean at—"

"I mean," said the colonel quickly, and rather more loudly, "at the place we met before, to sign documents."

"Oh," said Hugo. "Yes. I see."

"And a word to the wise. If you go out, keep your eyes open. I think it's very probable that you're being followed, too."

There was a click as he rang off. And—or was it Hugo's imagination?—a second click immediately afterward as though someone else had cleared the line.

He went downstairs to talk to his mother.

She said,"Your Uncle Howard had this complex, too. He was followed all the time. In his case it was little brown men. Once, in an Indian restaurant, he got it into his head that the waiter was going to throttle him. He hit him in the stomach with a half-full bottle of hock. There was a terrible fuss."

"I'm not sure that this is all imagination."

"It must be. People don't follow people around and listen on their telephones. Not in real life."

"There was no imagination about blowing up that car. And the two men who did it are still in England."

"How do you know?"

"If they'd tried to get out, they'd have been caught."

His mother sniffed.

The days that followed were uncomfortable. Hugo was unable to decide whether he was under observation or not. In a Tiger episode it had been easy. The camera had picked out the inconspicuous man in the raincoat doing nothing in a doorway and had tracked up on him with a single sinister note of music. Even the dullest viewer had grasped what was happening.

Without such assistance it was more difficult. In one way or another the conduct of almost everyone seemed to him suspi-

69

cious. Might the dark complexes which had gripped his Uncle Howard have him in thrall?

It was almost a relief when, at the end of the second week in April, a week of high winds and lashing rain, on his way home after dark, he spotted an unmistakable movement in the bushes near the door on his side of the house. No doubt about it, a man was standing there.

The tensions of the past days were released in one tigerlike bound. The man half turned, stuck the point of his elbow into Hugo's stomach, winding him, and said, "That's no way to treat your partner, Mr. Greest."

"Sorry," said Hugo, who was still having difficulty with his breathing. "Didn't recognize you."

"I thought I'd wait for you to turn up," said the colonel. "I didn't want to disturb your mother. I came to tell you that the stuff is all safely aboard. I've got the documents here. You can cash the first letter of credit as soon as the bank opens tomorrow."

Part Two / Matériel

Chapter 9 / Martin Cowcroft and Charlie Wandyke

Hugo was dreaming.

He was in the engine room of a liner. He had dressed for dinner in full evening dress—stiff shirt, white waistcoat, white tie, and all—and he was beginning to feel the heat. He wondered if he could possibly take off his waistcoat but realized that this was going to be difficult. His hands were covered with oil. Or was it blood? As he woke up, he was saying to himself, very seriously, "Is it blood?"

The rumbling of the liner's engines was the ineffective old air-conditioner bumbling away in the window of his bedroom. The heat was real.

He got up, switched off the air-conditioner, and opened one of the side vents. It was six o'clock and the sun was well up. One or two dogs were wishing each other good morning. His second-floor flat looked out over the dhow harbor. There was a wisp of smoke going up already from the deck of each anchored vessel as breakfast was cooked. The sea was like blue-gray oil paint.

He got back onto his bed, pulled the sheet over him, and reflected on the events of the past twenty-four hours. The departure from Heath Row, the arrival at Bahrain. The transfer to a much smaller aircraft. The first sight of Umran, as daylight was fading: a sandy peninsula jutting away to the north, its spine formed by the darker brown of the Djebel Gozo. The landing on the short airstrip outside Mohara-el-Gib, the walk in the dusk to the ramshackle air terminal building.

Here he had met Martin Cowcroft.

Hugo folded his hands under his head and thought about Martin Cowcroft. It was clearly going to be of importance how he got on with him. He wondered whether he liked him. He was not sure, but he thought on the whole, and judging by first impressions, that he did.

Cowcroft was a good deal older than Hugo, but his lizard face gave no clue to his age. Hair, skin, and clothes had been bleached by sun and wind. He looked like a strip of seaweed which had been too long out of water. The only touch of color about him was the red and black brassard on his right arm. For he was the commandant of the Umrani paramilitary police force.

He had seen the baggage stowed safely in the back of the sand-colored Land Rover which was the only vehicle on view outside the airport, and gestured to Hugo to get in.

"Kind of you to meet me," Hugo said. "There seems to be a shortage of taxis."

"The riots made them scared to come out after dusk," said Cowcroft. "Taxi burning is a great crowd sport round here. Shop looting, too."

They were driving down a long straight empty road into the town. Most of the shop fronts were protected by heavy double-padlocked roller-steel shutters. The ones that had no shutters had little glass left in the windows..

"It seems quiet enough now," said Hugo.

"Until next time," said Cowcroft sourly.

Another Land Rover was coming toward them. It had three men in it, and two machine guns. One was mounted to fire forward; the other, operated by the man in the back, was on a swivel mounting with a three-quarter arc of fire to the rear.

All three men saluted. Cowcroft waved them to a halt, stopped his own car, got out, and went over. He seemed to be angry about something.

When he got back, he said, "If I've told them once, I've told them a hundred times. The man driving the vehicle must *not* salute. They're lousy drivers anyway. I used to have just the same trouble in India. I remember a Sikh sergeant trying to salute me when he was riding a bicycle *and* carrying a basket of eggs. Here's your quarters. You're on the second floor. I'll give you a hand up with the luggage. There's a government car for you. It's in the garage at the back. Here are all the keys. There's some cold food and beer in the refrigerator. I've got an Indian cook for you. He's a fat thief, but he does know how to make curry. I'll be pushing off now."

Yes, on the whole, he thought he could get on with Martin Cowcroft. Taverner had already filled him in on his background. He had been in the Indian police in the thirties. After that particular job had folded up, he had had a number of posts, as assistant political agent and suchlike, up and down the Gulf and had finally cast up, a piece of jetsam from the old colonial empire, on the remote shores of Umran. "He's like a salamander," Taverner had said. "He comes to life in the heat. One winter in England would surely finish him."

Hearing sounds which he took to be his cook arriving, Hugo decided to get up.

After breakfast he went down to look over the car. It was a respectable middle-aged Humber. He drove out north in it, along the coast road, to pay his respects to the ruler.

Daylight had brought out some traffic. There were a number of cars, most of them newer, shinier, and faster than Hugo's. There were carts pulled by donkeys, some driven by old men with beards, others by small boys. There was a herd of camels grazing on what looked like a crop of small dry thistles. The road, which followed the line of the coast, was a good one, with two lanes and a paved surface.

About five miles out, there was a byroad inland to the left. A signpost showed some words in Arabic which Hugo translated as "Township of Hammuz." He remembered Taverner talking about Sheik Hammuz and "younger brother trouble," and wondered if the two things were connected.

The best map he had been able to get hold of was a twenty-year-old admiralty chart. This showed the road he was on and the left-hand fork as dotted tracks, but this was not surprising. The roads looked newer than the chart. He spread it out on the hood of the Humber and tried to get his bearings.

Immediately out to sea was a chain of four little islands, which the chart called "the Ducks" and which did, indeed, look like a mother duck with three babies in line astern. Five miles behind him was the town of Mohara el Gib, which he had just left. Three miles ahead of him, up the coast, was a cluster of buildings which must constitute the royal palace. Apart from this, the map was almost as blank as an ancient cartographer's idea of Central Africa. The only genuine road which was shown on the map ran across the base of the peninsula from Mohara to the coast on the other side and down the coast (he guessed) to Ras al Khaima. There was a tiny unmarked clump of buildings at the point where this road turned, which might be the Hammuz of the signpost. The rest of Umran seemed to be mountain in the middle and desert all round it. Not an over-populated country.

He got back into his Humber and drove on toward the palace. It had been built as much for defense as for residence. A high crenelated and loopholed wall surrounded a considerable courtyard. Entrance was by a deep archway surmounted by bartizans, with an outer door, an inner door, and a gallery round the top from which attention could be paid to any unwanted visitors temporarily trapped between the doors.

Hugo drove through and parked his car beside a gun. He examined the inscription on the breech block and made out that it was of Turkish manufacture and date-marked 1908. He was wondering how this venerable piece of artillery could have reached Umran when he realized that someone had approached softly and was standing immediately behind him. It was a very large Arab, in the khaki uniform of the palace guard, who introduced himself as Major Youba and escorted Hugo into the presence of his employer.

He found Sheik Ahmed in a small room off the main majlis hall, with Prince Hussein and Sayyed Nawaf. All three rose to greet him and shake him by the hand. After ceremonial coffee had been brought in and poured from a brass pot into tiny cups —bitter but not unpleasant—the meeting proceeded to business. Hugo spoke in Arabic, stumbling occasionally over a technical term but finding the words coming back to him with surprising fluency.

76

"I understand," said the ruler, "that all my arms left London by ship last Monday."

"All except the tracked vehicles. They are being picked up at Bari."

"Then they should be at Beirut by the end of the week."

"Inshallah," said Hugo.

"All things are in the hands of Allah," agreed the ruler. "But here is someone who will be glad to see my beautiful toys when they do arrive."

It was Martin Cowcroft, in white ceremonial police uniform, white helmet, sword and all.

"I thought," said Hugo, "that your police were already fully equipped and that what was coming over now was for your army."

"Can't give them to one and not the other," said Cowcroft. "They'd be jealous as cats. A rifle out here is wife, family, and food."

"Then a machine gun must mean polygamy," said Hugo.

This had to be translated for the ruler, who was delighted. "Indeed," he said, "a man with many shots in his gun will need many wives. But what the commandant said is true. First we give arms to those we trust, our own policemen. Then we give them to our army, who must be taught how to use them. We shall need instructors. You can obtain them for me from England?"

Hugo reflected that this was something which might have been thought of earlier. However, he said, "That should not be too difficult. With the reduction of our own regular army, there should be quite a few NCOs who would jump at the job. We have a nucleus of them down in Oman already."

Shortly after this, the arrival of scented water and a brazier announced the end of the audience.

When they got outside again, Cowcroft said, "First thing I'd better do is take you out to see a compatriot of yours. He'd welcome the sight of another white face."

"Who's that?"

"His name's Charlie Wandyke. He comes from Lancashire. He's running the Metbor diggings. He's the most important man in the state right now. It's because of what he's getting out of that hole in the ground that we can afford all these new toys. We'll go in my Land Rover. Your Humber wouldn't appreciate this section of the route."

North of the palace, the road deteriorated. It was now a winding and at times undefined track between outcrops of rock, wandering inland when the going along the coast became impossible, veering out again as the rugged mass of the djebel forced them back toward the sea.

It grew steadily hotter. Cowcroft's reaction to this was to remove his helmet. "Wonderful climate," he said. "I haven't had a day's illness in five years."

"Wonderful," said Hugo, mopping the sweat from his forehead. It seemed to have got mixed up with a lot of dust thrown up by the Land Rover's wheels.

"Not much further now."

They turned a corner and Hugo saw a high barbed-wire fence ahead of them. A man who was squatting beside it approached them. His rifle was slung round his shoulder. The police sergeant who was driving the Land Rover braked sharply and they skidded to a halt.

"Tight security," said Cowcroft.

He produced a pass which had his photograph on it. The man examined it closely, then looked at Hugo. Cowcroft said something in an argot which Hugo could not follow. The man hesitated for a moment, then grunted, turned on his heel, unlocked the padlock which secured the gate, and held it open for them.

"I don't think that's tight security," said Hugo. "Suppose we had been saboteurs. Couldn't we have rushed him, taken his keys, and let ourselves in?"

Cowcroft grinned and said, "You might have been lucky. I shouldn't care to try it myself." He was looking up as he spoke and Hugo saw what he had missed before—a platform on wooden stilts, masked against the bushy slope. On the platform was a machine gun. The man behind it saw Cowcroft grinning and grinned back, a flash of white teeth in a dark face.

"I see what you mean," said Hugo thoughtfully.

They drove for a hundred yards down a gentle slope and

drew up in front of a T-shaped formation of wooden huts. A man came out. He was wearing a rather grubby bush shirt, khaki shorts, and desert boots. His face was red and his sharp nose was redder still, and peeling. He had a sun helmet on the back of his head.

"Good morning, Charlie," said Cowcroft. "I've brought Mr. Greest out to see you. He's our new military adviser."

"Pleased to meet you," said Mr. Wandyke. "I've got a feeling that military advice is just what we're going to need soon. Bags of it. Come inside."

The office was air-conditioned and was agreeably cool. The table in the middle was littered with papers, drawings, plans, books, and coffee cups. A bookcase behind the head of the table was crammed with books. When Hugo got near enough to them to read the titles he saw that they were mostly detective stories and Westerns.

"I thought we ought to begin Mr. Greest's education—" said Cowcroft.

"You can begin it by calling me Hugo."

"—Hugo's education by showing him what you're up to out here, Charlie."

"Haven't I met you somewhere before?" said Wandyke.

"Only if you watch television."

"Of course. You're the Tiger."

Cowcroft looked blank. He said, "What Tiger?"

Hugo had long ago got hardened to this sort of thing. He said, "It's a television series. Half-hour thrillers. It's been going for some time."

"Do you mean to say you've never seen the Tiger on television?"

"It's some time since I was last in England," said Cowcroft. "All we get out here are programs relayed from Saudi. Dancing girls and French films. Do you mean you're an actor?"

"I've been a number of different things," said Hugo. "An actor is what I was last."

"Think of that," said Cowcroft. He sounded neither pleased nor disappointed. "Fire ahead, Charlie."

"What would you like me to tell him?"

"Tell him everything."

"Everything?"

"The whole lot. Ruler's instructions."

"If you say so," said Wandyke. "As long as you realize that what I'm telling you is so far known only to Martin here and the ruler and the board of Metbor, and mustn't go outside that circle until we publish our report."

"Agreed."

"How much do you know about minerals?"

"As much as the average schoolboy."

"Do you know what nitrites are?"

"Not really."

"Then we'd better start at the beginning. Nitrites are minerals which only occur in places where rain has never fallen."

"Never?"

"Never, in geological time. There aren't many places like that. The deserts of Africa and Tarapacá in northern Chile, for instance. That's where most of the world's potassium nitrite comes from. This tiny patch of God's garden happens to be another one. Rain's pretty rare in these parts anyway. The maximum is around two good showers a year, which come across from Iran. They break on the djebel, and what water there is falls on the western coastal strip, where a bit of primitive farming goes on. It gives this patch a complete miss in bulk. All right so far?"

"I think so. No rain, therefore potassium nitrite."

"Not potassium nitrite. Much more exciting. Ytterbium nitrite."

Inspiration visited Hugo. He said, "Otherwise known as smitherite."

There was dead silence in the hut. Hugo looked up and saw that both men were staring at him.

"If you know nothing about minerals," said Wandyke, "where did you hear that name?"

"Colonel Rex—he's my arms contact man—certainly knew about it. But I'd heard it once before, too. I can't remember if it was Taverner at the F.O. or the ruler."

80

"Damn, damn, and damn," said Cowcroft. "The ruler's been shooting his mouth off. I was afraid something like that had happened when I saw those Yanks arrive."

"Is Ringbolt here?"

"He got in on Friday with a private army. And he's not the only one. Hammuz and that Iraqi jackal of his, Dr. Kassim, have been having a few unscheduled visitors in the last day or two. Envoys from Flag, I imagine. Where there's dirt, the dogs will roll in it."

Seeing Hugo look blank, he said, "Flag is the Federation for the Liberation of the Arabian Gulf. They're backed by the Chinese, and their roots are in the Yemen, but they're moving north. They've got a link with the Ba'ath party in Iraq, which is probably where Dr. Kassim fits in."

Hugo remembered Lord Twinley saying something like, "If I was a cartoonist I'd draw you a picture of little Umran with three suitors, each with a bouquet in one hand and a bomb in the other." He said, "What is it about smitherite that makes it so compulsively attractive?"

"Ytterbium is a fairly rare mineral," said Wandyke. "In every other case where it's been discovered, it's been in the form of ytterbium aluminium silicate. You can extract it, all right, but it's a difficult and expensive process. Here you've got it on a plate. Because it's in the form of ytterbium nitrite—that's to say in large globules, which can be separated by centrifuging. Which simply means twirling the stuff round until the heavier particles shoot out to the circumference. It's a simple and inexpensive operation which anyone can carry out. All right?"

Hugo said, "I understand that when you find ytterbium in this particular form you can get a lot more of it out a lot quicker and a lot cheaper. What I don't follow is why it's so important."

"Very simple. Scientists on both sides of the iron curtain have discovered that if you alloy titanium with ytterbium it increases its strength-weight ratio *and* approximately doubles its melting point. Titanium's the most important metal used in rocket construction."

They were halfway back to the palace when the police driver braked suddenly.

"What's up, Sergeant?" said Cowcroft.

The sergeant pointed to a spot ten yards ahead of them where there was a defile between two spurs into the djebel. When they were coming up the track, it had been in shade, but the sun had moved across now and the marks were quite clear. A vehicle of some sort had been driven up the defile.

The sergeant had got out and was sniffing at the tracks like a gun dog on a fresh spoor. He said, "Army truck. Four-wheel drive."

"It can't have gone far."

"Gone and come back again." The sergeant was on his knees, unraveling the marks. "Ten, twelve hours ago."

"We'll go on foot. Avoid messing up the signs." He looked out of the corner of his eye at Hugo and said, "You can come if you like."

"I'd rather come with you than sit here," said Hugo. The heat in the little amphitheater was ferocious. He plodded after them, up the defile. They kept well to one side, to avoid messing up the wheel tracks, which were clearly visible, coming and going. At the second bend, Cowcroft raised his hand to stop Hugo and the sergeant went forward alone. He shouted something and they followed him.

The body was tumbled among the bushes in a cleft in the rocks. No particular attempt had been made to conceal it. The

82

sergeant was on his knees beside it. He touched the head gently and it rolled round. The throat had been cut so savagely that the head had almost been severed from the body.

"It is Youssuf," said the sergeant.

The man was dressed in peasant clothes. His feet were bare. The swarm of flies which had been at work buzzed resentfully at the interruption.

Cowcroft was staring down abstractly at the body. He said to Hugo, "Youssuf was one of our men. He was working as a kitchen hand in Sheik Hammuz's palace," and to the sergeant, "They tortured him before they killed him."

The sergeant said, "They broke up his feet."

Hugo could see, now, the splintered ends of bone sticking out through the skin.

"He would not talk," said Cowcroft. "Whatever they did to him, he would say nothing."

Hugo tried to visualize what it would feel like to have your feet smashed up with a hammer, and quite suddenly the whole thing became too much for him. The blackened blood, the greedy flies, the heat, the smell, and his own imaginings came on him together, the earth and the sky changed places, and he was on his back, propped up against a rock in the shade, with Cowcroft forcing some brandy down his throat from a hip flask.

He put it aside and climbed shakily to his feet. He was angry, and his anger cleared his head quicker than brandy.

He said, "A bloody fine show. I'm meant to be your military adviser, and I pass out at the sight of blood."

"I expect it was the heat," said Cowcroft. "Let's get back to the car. I'll leave the sergeant here to see that no one disturbs things until we can get a party out."

Back at the Land Rover, he switched on the wireless and spoke into it at length. Then he got behind the wheel and they drove back toward the palace.

Hugo said, "I think you'd better put me in the picture about one or two things. You mentioned Sheik Hammuz. He's the ruler's brother, isn't he?"

"His younger brother, by eleven months."

"And you had a man planted to spy on him. Why?"

The Land Rover had traveled some distance before Cowcroft answered. Then he said, "It sounds a bit odd when you put it that way. But there are two factions in this country, and always have been. The eastern seaboard is the progressive side. It's got Mohara, which is the only town worth dignifying with the name. And the main dhow harbor and the boat jetty and the best roads, and now it's got the airstrip, too. The other side's primitive. Jungly, we should have called it in India. There's a bit of farming along the coast. Most of the farmers dabble in smuggling as well. The rest of them live in the desert or up in the djebel. The hill men are a pretty wild lot. When a light plane belonging to one of the local oil companies made a forced landing there last year, they rescued the four men in it all right. Then they sold them back to the company for eight thousand pounds. A thousand pounds a leg was the way they put it."

"And the company paid up?"

"Certainly. They didn't want a first installment of legs delivered. They paid up and kept quiet about it."

"And Sheik Hammuz, the ruler's brother, is a westerner."

"He's their tribal chief. Chief smuggler, principal brigand, and—by God, here he is."

They had swung round the last corner and were turning into the palace entrance. Just inside the double gate an enormous six-seater Cadillac was parked. It was painted dark red and was flying a blue and yellow flag on its hood.

Cowcroft parked his dusty Land Rover beside it. It was like a tramp steamer mooring alongside a battleship.

"Come on," he said. "Let's go in and see what the bugger's up to now."

84

Chapter 11 / The Americans Give a Party

Sheik Hammuz bin Rashid bin Abdullah was seated next to the ruler, his brother. He had the thin, prowlike nose which was the hallmark of the Ferini family, but he was clean-shaven. This surprised Hugo, who knew that among the desert Arabs for a leader not to wear a beard was a sign of eccentricity, if not of actual effeminacy. He wondered if some glandular trouble might have been at the root of it. It was unfortunate that this lack of hair should have revealed so nakedly the pendulous cheeks, the full lips, and the rounded dimpled chin.

A slight, pretty young man wearing an incongruously well-cut lounge suit was standing beside Sheik Hammuz. Hugo put him down as a Syrian or Lebanese, but was wrong on both counts. For this was Dr. Kassim, and he was a full-blooded Iraqi.

The ruler effected the introduction. Sheik Hammuz did not rise, but waved a fat, heavily ringed hand in Hugo's direction. Kassim said, "His Excellency is glad to see you here, Mr. Greest, and hopes that you will be able to work for the good of all."

"I hope so, too," said Hugo.

"You have seen the mining camp?" said the ruler.

"We've seen something else," said Cowcroft abruptly. "There's a dead man in the djebel, five miles north of here."

"An accident?"

"Not unless he cut his own throat accidentally."

"Tell us."

Cowcroft told them what he had found. When he described the injuries to the man's feet, Kassim said, "That would no doubt be robbers. They would torture him to reveal where he hid his money."

"Odd sort of robbers," said Cowcroft. "They were driving a standard army truck. We traced it back as far as this palace."

"And further?"

"After this it's a paved road. A truck will leave no traces."

"A pity," said Kassim. "For it will make it very difficult to trace the murderer."

"Army trucks with these particular tires aren't common," said Cowcroft.

This produced a moment of silence, but no other reaction.

"I am sure," said the ruler, "that you will do your best to discover the murderers, Commandant. When you discover them, they shall be condignly punished."

They took this as dismissal. When they got outside, they found the sergeant talking to Major Youba.

The major said, "Some of my men heard a truck drive past here just after midnight. They assumed that it was going back to the diggings. It returned about half an hour later. This was curious. It could not have reached the diggings and returned in that time, so what was it doing? They listened to it drive off down the road. They thought that it turned off the road towards Yammuz."

"Could they conceivably hear that?" said Hugo. "It's all of three miles to the turning."

"On a very still night."

"I don't believe it," said Hugo. "If they heard that truck turn off the road, it turned off somewhere before that road junction."

"It is possible," said Major Youba. "There is a track. It makes a shortcut back to the Yammuz road."

"Let's have a look at it," said Cowcroft.

The track went off to the right about a mile from the palace. The marks of the tires were quite plain.

"Bloody impertinence," said Cowcroft. "They didn't mind what traces they left. All they cared about was getting home to bed. We'll have a look at the other end. Better go by road, then we shan't spoil the trail."

They drove to the road junction, turned right toward Yam-

86

muz, and found the exit point of the track. The tire marks were there, plain as the pugs of a tiger making his insolent way to his cave after a night's hunting.

As they were examining them, the huge Cadillac came purring up the road behind them, checked its speed, and drove on. Sheik Hammuz and Dr. Kassim were sitting together in the back.

"Holding hands," said Cowcroft. "What a sweet pair. We shan't get anything more out of this. And if we go down to Hammuz and start asking questions, we'll have a riot on our hands. Get into my car. One of my men can take yours. There are several things I'd like to talk about."

However, they were in the outskirts of Mohara before Cowcroft spoke again. Then he said, "In the course of a long life, I've met a lot of nasty people. Chinese pirates, Afghan mullahs, African witch doctors, fakirs and fakers. But I'd give that Kassim three-star rating in any company."

"I didn't much like his looks," agreed Hugo. "He seems rather young to be a hardened villain."

"By the record, he's twenty-five. And he's packed more villainy into that quarter of a century than most people could get through in a lifetime. He's been an active member of the Ba'ath party since he was a boy. He was twelve years old when he carried the bomb, in a school satchel, that failed to kill King Hussein of Jordan and blew three of his bodyguard to shreds. He was in prison before he was fourteen, and got out by seducing the governor. He disappeared for a bit after that, and was thought to have been in Egypt. He was next heard of in the American University at Beirut, where he got a doctorate in zoology, and was sacked for masterminding a riot which ended in the principal's house being gutted. When the dust had died down, he came back to Iraq and was involved in the unsuccessful July coup. He came out the right side of that and was allowed, as a reward, personally to execute three of the colonels involved. It's commonly believed that he copied Himmler's favorite method, and had them strung up with a butcher's hook through the point of the jaw."

"You seem to know a lot about him."

"It's my job to know about these things," said Cowcroft. He addressed the sergeant: "Block ahead. Watch it."

The street they were in was congested with cars, carts, and bicyclists. Something seemed to have happened. Horns were blowing and people were shouting.

The sergeant swung the car to the right, down a side street between market stalls, then left into an alley so narrow that they seemed to be scraping the walls on either side, and out into an open dusty space where half a dozen boys were playing football. They crossed the pitch, interrupting a nice solo dribbling effort, bumped along a second alley, and came out into a broad road running west out of the town.

"Never stop behind a traffic block," said Cowcroft. "It makes things too easy for the man on the roof with a rifle."

"Do you mean it was a put-up job?"

"Probably not. But it doesn't pay to find out." They were running alongside a high white wall with occasional barred windows in it and a sprinkling of broken glass along the top. The gateway at the far end had a bar across it and there were two sentries on duty. One of them saluted. The other raised the bar and they drove in.

"There's an office next door to mine. I'd be happy for you to use it. The alternative would be to work from your own flat, but you might find this more convenient."

"It's very kind of you," said Hugo. "I'd been wondering just how I was going to work. I think this would be a very convenient place."

Safe, too. The thought of high walls, barbed wire, and armed sentries had suddenly become important.

"We've got good communications here. Anything important, we wireless it to the oil company in Bahrain on a private wavelength and they very kindly send it on for us. There's a land line, too. But that's apt to get blown down or rooted up. Letters go by airmail. But as we're not on a scheduled route, that's apt to be uncertain."

It was a nice room. It had a table and several chairs and an air-conditioner which worked a good deal better than the one in his bedroom. The table had been thoughtfully furnished with a clean blotter, a quantity of paper, and a pen set marked "With the compliments of B.O.A.C." It occurred to Hugo, not for the first time but now more forcefully than ever, that he had not the faintest idea of what his job was supposed to be.

As though reading his thoughts, Cowcroft said, "There's one priority just at this moment. *Get those arms out here.* And instructors, if you can. But the arms are more important. These chaps live with rifles. It won't take them long to learn about machine pistols and mortars."

Hugo said, "It's Thursday today, April twentieth. If the boat's up to schedule, it's loading the vehicles at Bari now. It's due in Beirut on the twenty-fourth. Colonel Rex is out there now."

"He's your partner?"

Hugo nearly said yes, and then reflected that the word had awkward connotations. He said, "He's the man who's helping with the buying and transport."

"In that case," said Cowcroft, "I suggest that your first message to him need only consist of one word. 'Dedigitate.' "

Hugo went home to lunch, driving his own car and meeting no traffic blocks. The streets seemed almost deserted. The heat was formidable, but not overpowering. That would come later, in July and August, with the maximum humidity which made the Gulf, in high summer, one of the least tolerable places on God's earth.

His cook had prepared a meal of stewed chicken, figs, and rice, which Hugo ate with little appetite. He then turned on the air-conditioner full belt, until it sounded like a powerboat at the climax of an exciting race, took off most of his clothes, pulled a sheet over himself, and slept surprisingly well.

When he woke up, it was dusk. Apart from a dry mouth and a faint aftertaste of figs, he felt surprisingly fit. He remembered this phenomenon from his time with Professor van der Hoetzen. As long as you could actually sleep in the afternoon, you could defeat the hot weather. He got up, had a shower, the water coming out tepid from the cold tap, put on a clean shirt, and wondered how he was going to spend the evening.

At this point his doorbell rang, and Hugo walked down the

small front hall to open the door. In the few seconds which it took him to reach the door, a complete sequence recorded itself in his mind. The Tiger, alone in his apartment in Hawaii (Saigon, Hong Kong, Berlin, Ankara, Mayfair, Bangkok). A ring on the doorbell. He goes to open it. The foot pushed into the door. The heavy character outside. This is a gun, see. Make a wrong move and you're dead, see. So take it easy.

Hugo opened the door. Outside, looking cool, relaxed, and happy, was Tammy.

"Say you're glad to see me," she said.

"I'm glad to see you," said Hugo. He took both her outstretched hands in his and, since she seemed to expect it, kissed her gravely, first on the right cheek, then on the left. Tammy growled and said, "That's what you do to all your girls."

"It's in my contract," said Hugo. "At the beginning of the script I kiss them in a fatherly manner. At the end, once, warmly, not passionately, but more in the manner of a brother greeting his sister after a long absence."

"Boy, would that be worth waiting for. I've come to invite you to a party. A housewarming, sort of. We've taken over the next house."

She led the way downstairs, along the pavement, and up a precisely similar flight of stairs next door. The equivalent of what would have been Hugo's front door stood hospitably open, and he could hear the sound of music. There were two men in the room. Bob Ringbolt switched off the record player and said, "Good to see you, Hugo. Let me introduce you. Bill Birnie, otherwise known as the Bulldog." This was a man with an elastic face and the build of a weight lifter, who grinned amiably. If he'd had a tail, Hugo felt sure he would have wagged it.

"Let's have a drink," said Ringbolt. "We can offer rye, on or off the rocks, gin and tonic, or brandy and ginger ale."

Hugo said, "You're better equipped than I am. In my flat the choice is orangeade or tea. I'll have the rye, if I may."

"We've been here a week now. And we're beginning to find out the local form. There's a character with one eye who has a store opposite the boat jetty. He's called Moharram—that's

90

roughly what it sounds like. He'll get you anything you want, from slave girls to pink champagne."

"I must look him up," said Hugo. "Cheers!"

"To our special relationship," said Tammy with an alley-cat grin, and sat down beside him on the sofa.

"What do you make of the setup here, Hugo," said Bob, "or haven't you had time to size it up?"

"It's like a story out of the *Arabian Nights*," said Hugo. "The wise and benevolent ruler, his wicked brother who wants his throne, and nasty Uncle Abanazar, dropping poison into the brother's ear."

"Abanazar? You mean Dr. Kassim."

"Is he really a doctor?" said Tammy.

"He's a doctor of zoology of Beirut University and a professional killer."

"I must get to know him better," said Tammy. "I just adore killers."

Bob said, "My guess is that he's Sheik Hammuz's boyfriend. I'd wager he's a raving old queer. When Moharram was talking about him, he called him—I can't give you the word in Arabic; it means 'half and half' and it's about the most insulting thing you can say about a man."

"All the same," said Birnie, "he'd fall in behind him quick enough if he won."

"That's right," said Bob. "That's all they're waiting for. To see who wins."

You too, perhaps, thought Hugo.

More drinks were brought. He noticed that Birnie seemed to have disappeared. Tammy's bare arm was pressed lightly against him. He could feel the warmth of it through the sleeve of his shirt. She was saying, "It's a funny thing how people get ideas about each other. When I was a girl—"

"What are you now?" said Bob.

"You can keep out of this. I was talking to Hugo. When I was a girl, I used to think all Englishmen wore stick-up collars and striped pants and talked like they had hot potatoes in their mouths. All right, that was silly. But English people are just as silly about us. My kid sister Toni's at Southwestern. An English friend of hers said, 'I suppose you do nothing there but take drugs and join in campus riots.' Actually she's studying theology."

It was while he was enjoying his third drink that Birnie came back. He sat down on a chair in front of them and joined in the conversation. He wasn't naturally a conversationalist, and the effort was apparent.

Hugo dragged his eyes away from the attractive curve of Tammy's neck and took a quick look around.

Now Bob had disappeared. The bulk of Birnie was blocking his view on that side, and he hadn't noticed him go.

A natural explanation occurred to him.

He said to Tammy, "If you'll excuse me mentioning it, do you keep in this place what we should call a lavatory, and you, I understand, refer to as a john?"

"Only low-class people call it that. And it's through that door at the end of the passage. Birnie will show you."

"I can find it," said Hugo. He moved quickly enough to forestall Birnie, and was in the passage before they could protest. There were two doors on the right. He opened the first one quietly and looked in.

The room was a bedroom. There was a packing case at the foot of the bed, and on it was an apparatus in an odd-shaped container with dials and lights on the front. A month earlier he would not have recognized it, but his knowledge of army equipment had now been considerably enlarged. It was a No. 19 transmitter-receiver wireless set.

Bob was wearing a headset and had his back to him.

Hugo closed the door as quietly as he had opened it.

Chapter 12 / Sheik Hammuz Keeps
His Options Open

Friday, being the Muslim Sunday, was an off day. Hugo woke late, chased away the lingering taste of rye whisky with a cup of coffee, cut himself a packet of sandwiches, and put the rest of the milk and coffee into a Thermos flask. Then he got out the Humber and drove along the waterfront, heading south.

The road started as a paved highway but deteriorated quickly into a rough but motorable track. About ten miles south of Mohara, a concrete post stood sentinel on either side of the track. Hugo gathered, from the inscriptions on them, that they marked the frontier between Umran and Oman. There was nothing else. The formalities of frontier posts and customs had evidently not yet reached this remote corner of the globe.

A mile further on, Hugo found what he wanted.

The track dipped toward the shore, and below it there was a stretch of empty white sand. He left the car on the last piece of hard and walked down onto the beach. There he found a hummock against which he could rest his back, spread a big towel, took off his clothes, and oiled himself all over. Then he lay on his back, roasting gently in the moderate oven of the April sunshine.

Half an hour of this would be as much as his body could stand. Half an hour of relaxed thought was what he badly needed. The last days had been so busy that he had lived, mentally, from hand to mouth.

Could it really have been as little as ten days ago when he had stood beside Colonel Rex, in the freezing mist, in London

Docks, watching the last of the big crates being opened up, inspected by the two duffel-coated government inspectors, nailed down, tagged, and swung into the hold of the S.S. *Lombardia?*

It seemed a lifetime ago, in a different world. The briefings with different departments of the Foreign Office. A visit to his dentist. The buying and packing of tropical kit and the dispatch into the blue of two heavy trunks which he had a feeling he would never see again. The telephone call from Sam, announcing that he had been offered the lead in the first out-of-London tour of a successful West End thriller. Turning down the offer. A second visit to his dentist.

Then there had been the very curious visit, after dark, to Queen Anne's Gate, when he had been admitted to one house and walked, by communicating doors, into the house next to it. There he had been received by a gray-haired, red-faced man with the look of a captain in the Royal Navy, who had given him a string of complicated instructions which had meant nothing to him at all.

He had never discovered the man's name.

Hugo rolled over to expose more of his left side to the sun.

Even though he had been in Umran for scarcely thirty-six hours, certain facts had become apparent to him. The most important was that no one, in the Foreign Office or the other curious departments which he had visited, had any real idea of what was going on.

Cowcroft could have told them. Why hadn't he? On the other hand, why should he? He was not employed by the British government. He was, like Hugo, a servant of the ruler.

"All the same," said Hugo to a large white bird with a red beak and a knowing yellow eye which was perched on a flat stone near him, "I think they ought to know, don't you?"

The bird winked at him, rose with a casual flip of his wings, and glided out to sea.

In the middle distance, shimmering in the heat haze, he could see the line of the islands which were called the Ducks. The northern one, the mother Duck, was certainly large

94

enough to have some sort of gun emplacement built on it and a heavy gun mounted. But would this be enough to block the mouth of the Gulf? Hugo doubted it.

Little though he knew of modern armaments, he did not believe that a gun, even a large gun, mounted on the mother Duck could seriously inconvenience an oil tanker creeping down the coast of Iran, more than thirty miles away, and hidden, as now, in the haze. The only things which could effectively dominate that outlet were a battleship or a squadron of dive bombers. A single aircraft carrier could do the job most economically. But the ruler, wealthy though he now appeared to be, could hardly be in the market for an aircraft carrier.

He thought he would have a bathe.

The water was tepid, and he had to walk a long way out before it was up to his shoulders.

It was six o'clock and the sun was beginning to throw long shadows down the sand before Hugo reinserted his salted and sun-reddened body into its clothes, made his way to his car, and drove slowly back toward Mohara.

He was in the outskirts of the town when the police car came rocketing out of a side road, spotted him, and jerked to a halt with a squeal of badly adjusted brakes.

Hugo recognized the sergeant who had been with them on the previous day. He seemed to be excited about something.

"Slowly," said Hugo. "Speak slowly."

The palace. He gathered the word "palace."

"I am wanted at the palace?"

"Quickly," said the sergeant.

Hugo drove along the northern road as fast as his Humber would go, which was not very fast. The police Land Rover kept up with him easily.

There was a roadblock at the last turning before the palace, but the sergeant shouted something and the heavy pole was swung aside. They sped on and turned into the gateway.

Cowcroft was standing in the inner entrance. He said, "Where the hell have you been?"

"Bathing."

"When you go out, do you mind letting someone know where you are? I've had half the police force looking for you."

"I'm sorry. Has something happened?"

"Yes," said Cowcroft. He turned on his heel and Hugo followed him across the courtyard. There was a raised veranda which flanked the main entrance to the palace and something was lying on it, covered by a white sheet. For a bad moment, Hugo thought it might be the ruler, but when the sheet was twitched aside he realized that it was a stranger. A bearded face looked up at him. The lips were drawn back in the grimace of sudden death. The middle of the body was black with blood.

"Who is it?" said Hugo. "What happened?"

"He came this morning with a message for the ruler. He was admitted, drew a knife, and tried to stab him. Major Youba, who was already suspicious of the man, was standing beside the ruler and shot him."

"He certainly shot him," said Hugo.

"He put a dozen bullets into him from a machine pistol. You can't take any chances with a homicidal maniac."

"Was he a maniac?"

"Self-induced mania. He was full of bhang. Look at his eyes."

The eyes were rimmed with red and there was a crust of dried foam round the lips.

"Who sent the man? Who organized it? What does it mean?"

Cowcroft replaced the sheet and stood up before he spoke. He said, "He has been identified. His name is Abdullah bin Zafra. He is related by blood to Raman bin Zafra, who commands one of the contingents in the bodyguard of Sheik Hammuz."

"Then it's a declaration of war."

"Nearly. But not quite. It will be too easy for Hammuz to say, if he wishes, that he knows nothing of the matter and regrets it deeply. It is well known that when men overuse hashish they lose control of their senses."

"*If* he wishes."

"Exactly," said Cowcroft. "He has kept all his options open."

Hugo drove home more slowly than he had come.

96

When he was shaving next morning, Hugo saw the ship arriving. It was flying the red ensign on the main and the zebra-striped flag of Umran at the foremast. He watched it being fussed into position, stern first, at the end berth by one of the port tugs. Remembering his experiences when bathing, he concluded that there must be a considerable dredged channel to allow in even such a moderate-sized boat.

After breakfast, he walked down the jetty to have a closer look at her. She was the S.S. *Lyne Bay*. The hatches were already off and a gang was busy slinging crates ashore. One had broken open. It seemed to have held tinned peaches.

A man who was leaning on the tail of the foredeck smoking a pipe spotted him and waved him to come aboard.

Hugo climbed the gangplank and introduced himself. The man with the pipe turned out to be the captain. He invited Hugo into the tiny stateroom and offered him a glass of the gin which sailors seem to drink at all hours of the day and night. Hugo settled for a lime juice. He judged from the man's accent that he came from the same county as Charlie Wandyke.

"Certainly I know Charlie," said the skipper. "We went to the same kids' school. You might say it's because of Charlie I'm here. Or put it another way: if it wasn't for him, I certainly wouldn't be here. The freight on those few cases of tinned fruit wouldn't pay the passage out. As soon as they're unloaded, the real cargo will be coming down."

"Smitherite."

"Is that the fancy name they have for it? I can tell you one thing about it. If it was gold dust they couldn't treat it more carefully. It comes down in sealed sacks; each is weighed to the last ounce. You saw that crate of tinned stuff they dropped, accidental on purpose, on the quay. That's winked at. They always drop one case. The gang look on it as their perks. But if they spilled a single pinch of what's in those bags, the foreman would have their hides off them."

"How much have you taken off so far?"

"This is my second trip. The *Morecamb Bay*—that's our sister ship—has taken one. That's three loads at a hundred tons a time. They bring it down in lorries. Thirty to forty lorryloads." He looked out of the porthole. "Here's the first of them arriving now. That's Charlie in the driving cab. Sit tight, I'll bring him aboard."

Charlie Wandyke came in looking dusty and worried, said yes to the gin, and perched on the table.

He said, "Looks as though you had some trouble at the palace. I noticed they'd doubled the guards and had roadblocks out. What happened?"

When Hugo had told him about it, he looked even more worried. He said, "We're out on a limb up at the diggings, you realize that? We're going to have to do something about it."

"You've got a contingent of armed police."

"Six armed policemen aren't much use against a hundred tribesmen. Mind you, they mayn't bother us at all. There's nothing much to loot. No. What I want is a motor launch, big enough to take all of us. When trouble starts, I'll shut down the diggings, put every man jack of us aboard, and go across to Iran until it's blown over."

"You're sure it is coming, then."

"It's almost here. Can't you feel a sort of prickling under your skin? Like when a bad storm's blowing up. You can feel it for days before." He drank some of his gin and said, "Why do you suppose Albert here stays on board instead of sampling the pleasures of the town?"

"Last time I came here," said the skipper, "I did make a round of the town. Indian sex films, bathtub liquor, and pox. It's not an experience I'd care to repeat."

Wandyke said, "I take it that's why you're moored stern first, with only two light ropes? And why you're keeping your crew on board?"

"I'm a naturally cautious man," said the skipper. "You always did look on the dark side, Charlie. I remember at school you wore a belt and braces."

"It's because I'm cautious," said Wandyke, "that I'm alive and healthy today. I was digging for wolframite in Kenya when the

98

Mau Mau trouble started. It was my first job, actually. I used to laugh at my chief because he kept an army jeep, fully tanked up, under his back porch, with his bull terrier sleeping in it. We got away in it with two minutes to spare and beat it for Nairobi. Some of the other teams weren't so lucky. The Maus jumped them at night. They cut off the hands and feet and heads of any white men they caught and threw the bits down the mine. We found them when we reopened the diggings."

"For God's sake," said the skipper. "Have another drink and cheer up."

Hugo had been doing some sums. He addressed Wandyke: "If you've only actually got out two shiploads of a hundred tons each so far, where's the ruler's money coming from?"

"You don't buy minerals by the pound like sugar. You sell production. When our first samples had been assayed in London, the ruler started selling forward on the London Metal Exchange. This stuff goes at around one thousand pounds a ton. That's nearly ten shillings for every pound of it."

"No wonder you're careful with it," said the skipper.

"It's a sizable lode. We're only beginning to scratch the edges of it. Sooner or later, one of the big metallurgical outfits from America or Germany is going to take it over and open it up properly. They'll build a dock alongside the diggings, big enough to take bigger boats than Albert's tub, and they'll put up a ropeway and run the stuff straight on board. That way they could bring out five thousand tons a month."

Hugo did some more mental arithmetic and said, "That's sixty million pounds a year."

"Right. And say a quarter, or maybe a third, goes away in expenses and freight. That leaves forty million, split equally between the company and the ruler. It puts him straight into the big league. Above Abu Dhabi, and not so far below Kuwait. As long as the ore lasts."

"And as long as he lasts," said the skipper. "We'd better see how they're getting along with this lot."

Hugo took this as a hint that the party was over. As he walked down the jetty, he looked with interest at the cargo which was coming on board. It was in stout plastic bags, each one folded over at the top and fastened with wire. The end of the wire had a metal seal on it. Each bag was being weighed before it was lifted on board, and the weight was being recorded by two men; one would be from the mine and the other would represent the shipping company. At fifty pounds a hundredweight, you couldn't blame them for being careful.

As he was leaving the jetty, he remembered that he had some shopping to do. He was planning a return party for his American colleagues. The first requisite would be rye whisky and the second some cans of beer.

The one-eyed Moharram greeted him warmly. There were no dancing girls or champagne on view, but there seemed to be pretty nearly everything else in that vast dim emporium, from gin to lavatory paper. When Hugo had chosen what he wanted, adding, as an afterthought, a tin of peaches which looked suspiciously like one of the ones he had seen on the quayside that morning, Moharram clapped his hands and a very old woman, dressed from head to toe in black, hobbled out of a back room, added up the score on a scrap of paper, accepted the pound notes which Hugo offered her, did a further sum, and gave him his change in Umrani royals.

Moharram said, "She's my mother. She calculates good."

"And where did you learn to speak English?"

Moharram grinned, exposing a fearful row of yellow teeth.

"No English. I speak American. Four years in America. In Brooklyn, New York. Fine people, the Americans. Lots of money. Very generous."

Very generous, agreed Hugo. If it had not been for American generosity, he would not have been there at that moment.

He dropped his purchases at his flat and drove out to the police fort. Cowcroft was waiting for him, with a message. He said, "It seems to be in some sort of code. I imagine it means something to you."

Hugo remembered that Colonel Rex had given him a code book with instructions as to its use, which he had understood only vaguely. He took it out of his briefcase and set to work. Half an hour of sorting out, with a dash of guesswork, produced: "Apples and oranges arriving Billingsgate on schedule twenty-fourth morning, Rex."

"That's the day after tomorrow," said Cowcroft. "If they air-freight them straight out, the first lot should be here by Monday evening. That should be all right. Things are a bit quieter now. I've got a feeling that attempt at the palace was premature. Anyway, a brotherly note of condolence and congratulation on his escape was delivered by hand this morning."

"You mean that Sheik Hammuz wasn't behind it?"

"I don't mean anything of the sort. I mean that it was bad timing. He must have intended the assassination to be a signal for general revolt. It went off too soon. Do you carry a gun?"

"No. Ought I to?"

"Up to you. Have you ever used one?"

"I've never actually fired one."

"I think it's time you started."

Cowcroft unlocked the big safe in the corner of his room, unlocked a drawer at the back of it and, after some thought, selected one of the five or six guns in it.

"Do you know what this one is?"

"Certainly. No one knows more about guns, in theory, than I do. It's a short-barrel version of the American Police Positive .38 revolver. The last person I shot with one was a Guatemalan drug smuggler. I hit him at twenty-five yards when he was running down an alleyway in the dusk."

"We've got our own practice range here," said Cowcroft. "Let's see what you can hit at ten yards in daylight."

Hugo spent the next half hour, under instruction from a police sergeant, trying to hit a target in the shape of a crouching man which sprang up from behind a barrier of sandbags. Every policeman who had nothing better to do came over to enjoy the fun.

At the end of the half hour, fifty rounds had been expended, Hugo's right wrist was aching abominably, and the target had been hit three times.

Cowcroft came across to watch. He said, "You're trying too

101

hard. You shouldn't aim with a handgun. You wouldn't ever have time, anyway. Try it by instinct."

"What do you mean, instinct?"

"Put the gun down a moment. Now, point your finger at my stomach. Quickly. Don't think about it."

Hugo did so. Cowcroft, who was standing ten yards away, looked at it critically, and said, "Do you realize that if your finger had been the muzzle of a revolver, you'd have hit me bang in the navel."

"Should I really?" said Hugo.

"Certainly. Now try it with the gun. Not at me. At the target. Hold it where you hold your hand, somewhere down by your hip. Arm bent, quite relaxed."

Five of the next six shots went into the target.

"Well," said Hugo, "if I'd known it was as easy as that . . . "

"The next thing is, how are you going to carry it? I think the old-fashioned shoulder holster is best. Don't forget to keep the safety catch on. And even more important, don't forget to take it off when you want to use it."

When Hugo drove out to the palace that afternoon, the weight of the gun, just above his left hip, was an unexpected comfort to him. He found the roadblocks removed and life going on much as usual. He reported to Sayyed Nawaf that the arms were on schedule and the treasurer looked relieved. He said, "We shall be very happy when they have arrived here safely."

Prince Hussein said, "You bring us arms. The Americans have brought something even more important." And when Hugo looked at him blankly, "A very lovely girl, don't you think so?"

"Oh, her," said Hugo. "Yes, she's quite a girl."

He was thinking of that comment that evening, as he was undressing to go to bed, when the doorbell rang.

Last time, it had been Tammy. He hoped it might be her again. He pulled on his trousers and coat and had started for the door when he remembered that he had left the gun and harness hanging on the chair beside his bed. After a moment's hesitation, he went back, feeling curiously shamefaced, and readjusted the harness.

102

The bell rang again.

Hugo walked to the door and opened it, keeping one foot behind it to prevent any sudden inward thrust.

It took him a moment to recognize Moharram. The storekeeper bowed and said, "Pardon the late call, Mr. Greest. I have a visitor at my store. He'd like a word with you."

Hugo said, "Come in. I shan't keep you a minute."

"That's all right, Mr. Greest. I'm quite happy to wait here."

"Certainly not. Come in. And shut the door. That's right."

Hugo went into his bedroom, leaving the door open, lifted the receiver, and dialed a number. Cowcroft answered him.

He said, "I've just had an invitation from a neighbor of mine, Moharram. He wants me to meet a man."

"Is that old Mo, who keeps the general store?"

"That's the chap. I expect it's quite all right. But would you ask one of your cruising cars to park outside his shop? If I'm not out in half an hour, they can come in and look for me."

Hugo heard Cowcroft chuckle. He said, "You've been watching too many television plays. All right, I'll get one of them on the wireless."

If Moharram had heard, and understood, this conversation, he showed no sign of it. He led the way down the stairs and along the pavement toward his shop.

A black Cadillac was parked outside. There was no one in it.

"Is that your visitor?" said Hugo.

When Moharram turned to answer, his face looked curiously livid under the overhead neon lights. He said, in a husky parody of his normal speaking voice, "That's him. He's a great guy. You'll see."

Hugo realized, with a cold feeling, that the old man was terrified. The shop, which had been badly lit before, was now in almost total darkness. A light showed at the far end, under the door of the room the old woman had come out of.

104

Hugo slid his hand inside his coat and touched the grip of the revolver. His heart was beating uncomfortably. Take it easy.

"You lead on," he said.

Moharram looked up at him.

"I said, you go in front."

Moharram nodded and bobbed off down the center aisle between the tins of fruits and jars of jam and bottles of tomato sauce. An ambush among the crates of oranges and sacks of potatoes at the far end? If it was, it remained unsprung.

Moharram held the door open. Hugo said, again, "You first."

The old man looked surprised, but went in. Hugo followed cautiously.

Behind the small, round, paper-cluttered table which occupied the center of the room, Dr. Kassim was seated in a wicker chair. He was smoking a cigarette in a long amber cigarette holder, and he was alone.

Hugo removed his right hand from inside his coat. The movement, though unobtrusive, did not escape Dr. Kassim. He said, "You are a cautious man, Mr. Greest. Do you always come armed to an interview?"

"When I have to meet an unknown person, in a strange place, in the middle of the night, always."

"But why? In this instance, if I had meant you any harm, and had brought a friend with me, he could have shot you with a machine pistol as you came through the door, as efficiently"— Dr. Kassim's thin mouth closed with a snap—"as efficiently as Major Youba shot the unhappy Abdullah."

"No doubt. And the noise would have brought in the two policemen who are sitting outside at this moment in a car. Possibly they, too, would have been armed with machine pistols."

"Excellent," said Dr. Kassim. "How comforting to meet someone who thoroughly distrusts you. It offers, don't you think, a firm basis for mutual understanding. Have a cigarette?"

"Thank you, no. You have some business you wished to discuss?"

"Business, of course. But to have the pleasure of making your better acquaintance, too. I am a great admirer of your performances, Mr. Greest. One word of criticism. When the Tiger came through that door, *he* would have kicked it open with his foot and fallen flat on his face. Then the hail of bullets which awaited him would have gone over his head. Lying on the floor, he would have whipped out his own gun"—Dr. Kassim suited the action to the word, and a black automatic appeared in his hand—"and shot down his opponents, one—two—three." As he said this, he pointed it in rapid succession at Hugo and at two imaginary opponents. "It is a rule of the cinema that only villains are hit by bullets. I fear that it is not so in real life."

The automatic disappeared as smoothly as it had arrived. Hugo said, in what he hoped was a steady voice, "These things are easier to arrange in the studio. Should we get on with our business?"

"Why not? I am a businessman. But I cannot talk business with a dry throat." He rapped out something, and Moharram waddled across to a cupboard and produced a full bottle of Haig, two glasses, and a bottle of soda water. Kassim mixed the drinks, and ostentatiously took a long pull out of his own first.

"In case you should suppose it to be drugged," he explained amiably. "To business, then. Let me start by clearing away some spiders' webs of fantasy. Has the ruler spoken to you about his plans for building an Army of Umran? A modern and well-equipped force to hold the balance of power in the Gulf. Controlling the traffic through the bottleneck at the entrance of the Gulf. Wooed by all the great powers. Respected by everyone. You realize that such talk is all moonshine? There is no reality in it at all."

"I think I had begun to arrive at the same conclusion."

"Good. Then we start from common ground. Allow me to refill your glass. The ruler has one object and one object only in acquiring those arms. To defeat his brother, Sheik Hammuz. Not merely to defeat him. To annihilate him. Without modern arms, he cannot do it. Hammuz commands the loyalty of the western tribes. They are the real fighters. The ruler has a police force, and the nominal allegiance of the townspeople of Mohara. An allegiance which, I can assure you, would be transferred overnight to Hammuz if he won."

106

"You are a supporter of Sheik Hammuz? You find him an attractive character?"

The ghost of a smile twitched at the corners of Dr. Kassim's mouth. It was hardly a smile. More an involuntary grimace which lifted, for a second, the curtain which experience had taught him to draw over the tortuous workings of his mind. Just so might Torquemada have smiled at a naïve question from one of his familiars; or Cesare Borgia at a comment on his choice of wines for dinner.

He said, "If you are asking me for my frank opinion of Sheik Hammuz, I will give it to you. He is a fat and unpleasant pederast. And I would add, Mr. Greest, that whatever gossip may say, I am not his sleeping companion. I would as soon copulate with a feather mattress. In any event, there are plenty of camel boys available when he feels that way inclined. No; considered as a man I rather prefer the ruler. He may be stupid, but he is a tolerable person."

"In that case, why do you have anything to do with Sheik Hammuz?"

"Because it is my considered opinion that he will be the winner. And in politics it is the first rule that you must be on the winning side."

"Is it so important who wins?"

"Do not pretend to be more stupid than you are, Mr. Greest. Of course it is important. It is the most important thing in the Middle East today. Whoever wins controls the mineral concessions. And those concessions will naturally go to the power that supports the winner. The American, Ringbolt, appreciates the position perfectly. You know, of course, that he is in wireless communication with the U.S. cruiser squadron in the Indian Ocean? There is a light cruiser within twenty-four hours' steaming of Umran at this moment. I do not, myself, think they will interfere. Gunboat diplomacy is too blatant for modern tastes. Although your own country used to indulge in it quite frequently."

"We used to," said Hugo sadly. "No longer. We're far too polite to hurt anyone's feelings now."

Dr. Kassim said, "That brings me precisely to my point. We

107

are both realists. It does not matter to us which of these two deplorable desert chieftains wins his private war. What does matter is that we should know, in advance, who the winner is going to be. Then we can anticipate, and share, the rewards of that victory."

"I'm not sure that I follow you."

"I think you do. But let me state it as a simple proposition. If neither side had modern arms, Hammuz would win. It would be an unspeakable contest. I have some experience of civil war, in Kurdistan. No quarter would be given, or expected. Prisoners would be tortured, before being released to death. Neither sex nor age would offer any hope of clemency. In such a war, ultimately the tribesmen of Sheik Hammuz would prevail. On the other hand, if the ruler had succeeded in arming his police and his private guard with modern weapons, it is they who would win. The war would be shorter, the casualties as great, but more quickly and efficiently achieved. You follow me?"

"Yes," said Hugo. "I follow you." He knew now what was coming and that foreknowledge allowed him to control his anger.

"Logically, therefore, the solution is to load the dice so that we know, in advance, on what side it will come down. Let Sheik Hammuz have the modern arms, and there can be no doubt at all who will win. In fact, there will hardly be any fight at all. It will simply be—"

"A massacre."

"One or two people will have to die. But there will be no general slaughter. It is only when one side wins *after* a bitter struggle that these things happen. You are not old enough to remember the Spanish Civil War. Nor am I, of course, but I have read of it. If General Franco had marched straight into Madrid and the war had been over in a week, do you think that a tenth—a hundredth—of the atrocities would have occurred? Of course not."

"What, exactly, is your suggestion?"

"It is very simple. Your arms, I am told, arrive in Beirut on Monday."

Hugo nearly said, "And who told you that?" But reflected that it was a pointless interjection.

"They are to come on here by plane. If the plane is to land on the primitive runway here at Mohara, it must be a comparatively light plane. It would be quite natural, therefore, for you and your colleagues in Beirut to arrange that the only convenient and available transport was by planes too large to put down here. The arms would therefore be landed at the nearest airport with a suitable runway, which is Fujaira. They would come on by road, in lorries or under their own power, along the coast, through Ras al Khaima, where they would turn inland and use the good road which runs along the southern part of Umran to Mohara."

"That sounds quite a feasible program," agreed Hugo.

"You will understand me when I say that at the point where the road turns inland, the convoy will pass within half a mile of the fort and headquarters of Sheik Hammuz. If it should happen to fall into an ambush, could you be blamed for the loss of arms?"

"And the escort?"

"In the face of overwhelming odds, one hopes that they would see the light and behave discreetly."

"And if I agree to this plan?"

"As soon as we have your agreement—I have it here in writing—signed by you, a sum of twenty-five thousand pounds, in any currency you care to nominate, will be placed to your credit in a bank in Switzerland. You will be able to confirm its arrival. At the moment when the arms convoy leaves Fujaira, you will receive a similar sum."

"And if I refuse?"

"If you refuse, Mr. Greest, I can promise you one thing. The arms will never leave Beirut. And I doubt—I very much doubt —whether you will ever leave Umran."

But it wasn't a question of leaving Umran. It was a question of getting out of that room. Having gone so far, having shown so much of his hand, could Dr. Kassim risk letting him go if he did not agree? It was clear that the doctor was much more expert with firearms than he was. He might, of course, pretend to agree, sign whatever document was produced, and repudiate it afterward, but such a course, as well as being distasteful, had its own risks.

"Well, Mr. Greest?"

"I'll think it over."

"The interval available to you for thought is unhappily very brief."

"I don't follow you."

"You follow me perfectly. I saw you debating the matter with yourself a moment ago."

"Well—" said Hugo.

Moharram put his head round the door. Dr. Kassim said, "Go away."

Moharram said, "If I do not open the door for them, they will break it down."

There was a splintering crash of wood and glass and the sound of running footsteps. Dr. Kassim held himself upright and rigid. It was the rigidity of a steel spring under pressure. For a breathless moment he seemed to be calculating angles and probabilities. Then Hugo saw him relax.

As the police sergeant burst into the room, Dr. Kassim turned his head, gave him a look which stopped him in his tracks, then turned back again to Hugo. "It seems that you will have an interval for deliberation after all," he said. "Perhaps you will give me your answer tomorrow."

"Perhaps," said Hugo.

The ruler said, his face dark with anger, "But it is intolerable. The man must be brought to judgment and punished."

"You realize that he'll deny every word of it," said Cowcroft.

"He cannot deny that he came to see Mr. Greest. There are witnesses of that."

Hugo said, "Both policemen saw him. And the storekeeper."

"If he was not plotting against me, why should he have come, secretly, at night to see Mr. Greest?"

"If my assessment of his character is right," said Cowcroft,

110

"he'll say that Mr. Greest sent for him and himself proposed a bargain."

The ruler said, "No one would believe it." But there was an edge of uncertainty in his voice.

"What really interests me," said Cowcroft, "is that statement he made about the arms shipment. What was it he said? That if you didn't fall in with his plans, he would see to it that the arms never left Beirut?"

"Something like that."

"The man's an Iraqi. No doubt he's got friends in Lebanon. I suppose he might be able to pull some strings."

The ruler drew himself up to his full height and said, "If this man interferes in any way with *my* arms, I will seek him out and destroy him. Even if it means war."

The streets of Beirut were designed for camel and donkey traffic. The advent of fifty thousand cars, all of them large and most of them badly driven, has produced a fair imitation of bedlam.

Bob Livingstone, captain of the S.S. *Lombardia,* relaxed on his back seat of the aged Mercedes taxi and enjoyed it. He was in no hurry. He liked Beirut. He liked the Lebanese, who tried so hard to be sophisticated and were really very simple. He liked the suicidal way they drove their cars, the vigor with which they swore at each other, the warm smile which flashed out when the swearing was over.

The *Lombardia* had docked early that morning. The unloading and the attendant formalities would take two days to complete, after which he would allow himself twenty-four hours of shore leave before he went on to Port Said to pick up the return cargo.

It had been a successful trip so far, and he was looking forward to his meeting with the gentleman who had telephoned to make an appointment with him at the Hotel Continentale. He was so pleased with himself that he allowed the taxi driver to charge him twice the proper fare for the journey from the docks, and even added a tip.

The hall porter at the Continentale said, yes, there was a Colonel Delmaison in the hotel. He would be found in suite sixteen, on the first floor.

Colonel Rex got up as Livingstone came in. There was a

bottle of champagne in a cooler on the table, with two glasses beside it. The colonel untwisted the wire, eased out the cork, and filled two glasses. One he handed to Livingstone. The other he took himself.

"A salute to a successful trip," he said. They clinked glasses. "How is the unloading going?"

"Up to schedule," said Livingstone. "The heavy stuff, which was deck cargo, is coming off first. It's all going straight into the transit warehouses at the airport."

"Excellent," said the colonel. He went across to the desk, took out a flat black briefcase, and extracted from it a checkbook. "I promised you a personal bonus, Captain, if you arrived on time." He was writing the check as he spoke. "No particular sum was mentioned. I hope you will think two thousand dollars appropriate."

"Very generous," said Livingstone. "There's just one thing. Could you let me have some of it in cash?"

"Why not? I don't carry a great deal of cash about with me. Would five hundred dollars meet the case?"

"Lovely. It's not that I'm worried about taking a check, you understand, but as soon as the cargo's landed, I'm planning to treat myself to an evening at the casino."

"The Casino du Liban," said the colonel. "Yes. Indeed, one of the finest in the world. But I am afraid that your five hundred dollars will melt there, like the snow you can see on the mountaintops."

"Melt or multiply," said Livingstone, "I shall enjoy every moment of it." He pocketed the five one-hundred-dollar bills which the colonel handed him, folded the check carefully away, finished his champagne, and took his departure.

After he had gone, Colonel Rex emptied his almost untouched glass of champagne down the basin in the bathroom. It was a drink for which he had little taste, for the cheap Lebanese variety least of all. However, the bottle would be a useful prop for other visits which he anticipated that morning. There would be visitors who might not be quite as easy to deal with as the simple Captain Livingstone. When the colonel consid-

113

ered the remote chance of the check for fifteen hundred dollars being honored by the Canadian bank on which it had been drawn, and reflected on the fact that in the financial statement which he was already preparing for his partner, Mr. Greest, the item "Bonus to Captain" would feature as five thousand dollars, he was not dissatisfied with his enterprise so far.

The rest of the morning was taken up with visitors of different sorts. There was a complicated air-freight schedule to arrange. There were insurance agents to deal with. There was even an enterprising journalist from the *Journal Libre du Liban,* to whom the colonel spoke of Arab solidarity and the need for the smaller states to arm against unspecified enemies.

After an excellent luncheon in the hotel dining room, the colonel locked the door of his room, wedged a chair under the door handle, took off most of his clothes, and went to sleep. He woke at dusk, shaved for the second time that day, took a shower, and was dressing when the room telephone rang.

It was the desk clerk.

The colonel said, "Ask Mr. Sharif to wait for five minutes, please, and then show him up. And would you please tell room service to send up a bottle of whisky, some clean glasses, and some ice."

The desk clerk said that he would see to it, and the colonel finished tying his tie. For the first time that day, he seemed thoughtful.

Mr. Sharif looked like a nice little cat. He had a head of smooth white hair, a round and cheerful face, and a multiplicity of chins which descended into the folds of his wide shirt collar. He shook hands gravely with the colonel, moved with soft-footed grace across the room, and accepted a glass of whisky, which arrived at that moment.

When the waiter had gone, there was a moment of silence. Colonel Rex said, "I had not expected to see you this evening."

"I had not anticipated that I should have to call on you," said Mr. Sharif. He, like the colonel, spoke in French.

"Has something happened?"

"Of that I am not sure. My business here is to watch over your

114

interests. I am what the Americans call a troubleshooter." Mr. Sharif smiled as though at a secret joke. "The way to shoot trouble is to see it coming and to destroy it before it arrives."

"That sounds like good policy to me," said the colonel pleasantly. "Do you see some cloud on the horizon?"

"Not a cloud. A man. He arrived from Baghdad this morning. He is known to be a member of the inner council of the Ba'ath party."

"Why should he trouble us?"

"I have an instinct in these matters. I had him followed from the airport. He went directly to the Ministry of Commerce. It was clear that he had an appointment with the minister. He was shown straight in. The meeting lasted for about an hour. When he came out, this man returned immediately to the airport. He will, by now, be back in Baghdad."

The colonel considered the matter. He respected Mr. Sharif's nose for trouble. He said, "The Ministry of Commerce controls export and import licenses?"

"That is so."

"We may be imagining things."

"I hope so," said Mr. Sharif. He refused a second drink and departed with the same inconspicuous grace.

The colonel finished his own whisky slowly. Then he corked up the bottle, put it into his briefcase, and went out, locking the door behind him. He deposited the key with the desk clerk and made his way through the dining room, out onto the terrace beyond, down some steps, across a courtyard, and into the kitchen quarters of the hotel. A man in a white apron who was working there looked up and saw the colonel but said nothing. The colonel walked across the room and let himself out by a door into a side street. Ten minutes of brisk walking, through a tangle of alleys and back streets, brought him out into Hamra Street, with its pizza bars, its pinball saloons, and its glare of neon-lit advertisements. The colonel glanced quickly to right and left, seized a half chance to dart across through the traffic, and disappeared once more into the obscurity beyond.

The apartment for which he was making had been found for

him by the faithful Mr. Sharif, and met his requirements exactly. It was inconspicuous, it could be approached from six different directions, and it had all the simple comforts which the colonel demanded.

These comforts included a little Lebanese girl called Fara.

Fara had dark brown eyes, long black hair, which she wore in a bun, and a figure which was beginning to spread a little. She swept and tidied the apartment, did the shopping, cooked and washed up such meals as the colonel ate there, and slept with him at night. She carried out all these functions efficiently and impassively.

The colonel sometimes wondered exactly what her status was. He paid her for board and lodging, and for other services. Terms were strictly cash, and payment in advance, but whether she kept the money for herself or passed it on to someone else was far from clear.

When he questioned Sharif on the matter, he said, "I think she is the owner of the whole house. Possibly of other houses in the neighborhood."

"There must be a man behind it somewhere. She'd need a protector."

Sharif had disagreed. He said, "Fara could deal with most situations herself. If trouble arose, there might be a father or a brother in the background. In Lebanon, family feeling is strong. But do not underrate her. She is a businesswoman first and last."

On the following morning, he was back in his hotel room in time for his early-morning coffee and croissants. It suited his plans very well that the world should suppose him to be staying at the Continentale.

His first visitor that morning was the area manager of Gulf Air Transport Services. He was a Scotsman, and he wasted no time. He said, "We've run up against a bit of trouble. The customs officer at the airport tells me we need a special export license before we can start loading the planes."

"But that's nonsense," said the colonel. "The cargo is in transit. It's in temporary bond only, in the transit warehouses."

"It may have come in without import license. It won't get out without an export permit."

116

"Why not?"

"They require a certificate of origin."

"Show them the bills of lading."

"It's not the country of origin they're worried about. It's the manufacturer. They've been informed that more than one of the suppliers is on the Israeli boycott list."

"Ah," said the colonel.

The cat was out of the bag now with a vengeance.

He walked across to the window and opened it. From his balcony he could look down across the terrace, at the blue-green sea tumbling white over the rocks. He needed time to think.

"You realize," he said, "that this is nonsense. I can produce a list of the factories or depots from which every item in that cargo was purchased."

"What they require is not a list but a certificate, from the company concerned, that all the items shown on the manifest as being bought from them actually originated in their own works. There have been a number of cases lately where the boycott has been evaded by Israeli-owned factories making the sale through an associated company that was not on the list."

"I could get them certificates, but it would take time."

"How long?"

The colonel considered the matter. The Spaniards would be the most difficult. It was even possible that they could not really produce a certificate. In any event, no one in Spain did anything today which could be put off until tomorrow. He shook his head angrily. "It's Tuesday today," he said. "The local letter of credit expires on Monday. It's quite impossible."

"Could you not get the time limit extended? Fifteen days. A week even."

"I could try," said the colonel. "Come back this afternoon and I'll let you know."

He booked a call to Hugo in Umran and spent the rest of the morning composing and dispatching telex messages to his suppliers, but he did it without conviction. The emissary from the Ba'ath had done his part too well. The dead hand of officialdom was not going to be lifted in six days.

117

At eleven o'clock Hugo came through. He listened to what the colonel had to say, and said, "I'll put it to Sayyed Nawaf. But I shouldn't think there's much hope. Things are hotting up here. The ruler needs those arms."

Just after midday, he came through again. He said, "Request refused. Absolutely and categorically."

"I suppose you realize what this means?"

"More or less."

"Then let me explain." The colonel was speaking deliberately in order to control his anger. "If we cannot load those arms and produce airway bills to the bank here next Monday, our letter of credit expires. We have purchased half a million pounds' worth of goods for which we have paid only a deposit. If the goods lie too long in storage here, the local authorities will impound them and sell them to defray storage charges. That will leave you and me owing the suppliers about four hundred thousand pounds, less any balance on the sale. Knowing how these customs auctions are rigged, I very much doubt whether there would be any balance. You understand the position?"

"I understand it," said Hugo. "But even if I was able to explain it to the ruler, I doubt if it would make any difference. If you mention any possibility of delay in delivering the arms, he simply doesn't listen."

"Couldn't you get it into his head that if we can't clear the arms he'll lose the twenty percent deposit he *has* paid?"

"I told him that. All he said was that if he didn't get the stuff early in May, it would be useless to him anyway."

"Why?"

"I can't explain," said Hugo. "At least, not on this line. But he's probably right."

"I see."

"Look, you've got to do something. Pull some strings."

"There's only one thing that pulls strings in this part of the world," said the colonel, "and that's money."

He said the same thing to Fara when he got back to his apartment that evening.

"Who's got all the money in Beirut?"

118

She said, "The Jannis have a great deal of money."

"Who are the Jannis? And what do they do?"

"They have the gardens. Up in Bekaa."

"Gardens?"

"Hemp gardens. Indian hemp."

"Oh, cannabis. I see." The colonel considered the matter. There would be dangers in dealing in such a market. And the operators would drive a hard bargain. But it sounded like the sort of money he wanted. He said, "How do I get hold of these people?"

"I will find out."

She was gone for an hour. The colonel spent the whole of the hour drinking whisky and wondering if he had been a fool. When she came back, she had an address scribbled on a piece of paper. She said, "You go to this place. You will need a taxi. It is a little way out of the town. You ask for the young Mr. Janni. You will say that you have come to arrange some insurance."

"Now?"

"Now, yes."

At the door the colonel said, "You didn't tell them I was staying here?"

Fara smiled. "Certainly not. If I had done so, they would not have thought you were a big shot. I told them you were living at the Continentale."

"You're a sensible girl," said the colonel.

He walked through half a dozen streets, doubling in his tracks, before he hailed a passing taxi and gave the driver the address. They had soon left the suburbs behind them and were climbing through twisting streets and round hairpin bends. Here the houses were larger and more scattered, and the street lamps few and far between. They turned into a broad avenue which ran out along the flank of the mountains. The house in front of which they stopped was solid, not pretentious. A large two-story villa, with white walls, tiled roof, and a deep balcony extending round three sides.

When the colonel got out of the taxi and the engine was switched off, he noticed how silent it was. His ears had got attuned to the roar of the city. Here it was so quiet that you could pick up the chirruping of the crickets and the love song which a nightingale was composing in a tree by the gate. Far below, Beirut lay spread out at his feet, a chaplet of lights flung around the bay of Saint George.

The driver said, "Lovely, eh? A fine city, eh?"

"I've seen a heap of cities," agreed the colonel. "I don't know a finer one." A practical thought struck him. "It won't be easy to find a taxi up here. Would you wait?"

"Ten pounds Lebanese," said the driver, also coming down to earth.

"I'll give you five dollars American. I won't be more than half an hour."

"O.K., O.K."

The front door was opened by a manservant whose tight-fitting white jacket showed off a fine pair of shoulders. He stood looking at the colonel, who said, "I have come about a matter of insurance." The man nodded, led the way down the passage, ushered the colonel into a sitting room, and went away. The colonel sat down and relaxed. He expected to be kept waiting. He would have done the same for anyone who came asking him a favor. Five minutes passed. Then a door at the far end of the room opened and a man came in. The colonel, who was accustomed to sizing people up, knew that he was in the presence of power and money. Before the man opened his mouth it had spoken from his easy manner, from his English-made clothes and shoes, from his heavy but not flabby face.

The colonel said, "I am unpardonably interrupting your evening, so I will be brief. I require ten thousand pounds, either in local currency or in dollars. I can offer, as security, approximately four hundred thousand pounds' worth of goods, in warehouse here in Beirut. The money would be repayable at the end of the month, before the goods leave the country."

"First, I should like to know who you are."

The colonel handed him his card. The man put it down on the table without looking at it. He said, "Your name I know already. I require to know the names of some people who are acquainted with you, in the way of business."

120

"Certainly. But they may not be known to you. Most of them are in Canada or America."

"I have friends on both sides of the Atlantic."

The colonel started to mention names. At the third one, the man said, "Yes, I know him. I will contact him tomorrow. If he gives me a satisfactory report, I will do business with you. But let me explain one point. I do not lend money; I use it to buy goods. I will buy ten percent of your cargo."

"Ten percent?"

"If what you tell me is correct, ten percent should be worth forty thousand pounds. I will buy it for ten thousand pounds."

"It's a hard bargain."

"Certainly. But then, I am well aware of the nature of the goods. They are not easily salable. And you must need the money very badly, or you would not have come to me for it."

"I ought to consult my partner. But there is no time, so I accept."

"Then we will meet in my lawyer's office tomorrow morning at eleven o'clock to sign papers. Here is his card. Please allow my chauffeur to drive you back."

"It's very good of you, but I kept the taxi."

"I sent it away," said the man. "My own car is outside. Where can he take you?"

"I'm at the Hotel Continentale."

"Yes, of course."

At half-past eleven on the following morning, the colonel walked out of the office of one of the leading Beirut notaries with a certified check for twenty-five thousand dollars. At a quarter to twelve he entered the main branch of the Arab Bank, where he changed the check into new notes of large denomination. In the course of the next hour he visited half a dozen different banks and changed these into older notes, of smaller amount. Then he telephoned Mr. Sharif from a call box and made an appointment to see him at six o'clock that evening.

The rendezvous, on this occasion, was the back room of a café in Martyr Square. Mr. Sharif brought with him a tall, silent man

121

who seemed, from the few words he let drop, to be a senior official in the customs service.

At the end of two hours of talk, Mr. Sharif said, "It can be done. It will mean sending the stuff off, in a number of loads, to Bahrain. In theory, it will still be subject to the anti-Israeli embargo, but once it is out of this country, and beyond the immediate control of the minister, there should be little difficulty. It would be sensible to send the small arms and ammunition first, since I understand that it is in respect of them that a certificate of origin will be the most difficult to obtain."

The colonel nodded. He said, "When can you get the first plane off?"

The tall man said, "Not before tomorrow evening. Some repacking may be necessary."

The colonel took down a calendar from the wall. Under the date Monday, May 1, he drew a thick line in red.

He said, "I will pay half the agreed sum now. The other half provided that the last consignment is out of this country by this date. Can that be guaranteed?"

"All things are with God," said the tall man.

Chapter 15 / Reconnaissance in Force

On Wednesday morning, a council was held at the palace. It was clear to everyone present that it was a council of war.

On the ruler's right sat his uncle, the venerable Sheik Fayad bin Abdullah al Ferini. Hugo gathered that should anything happen to the ruler, Sheik Fayad would be regent until Prince Hussein was old enough to rule. Hussein sat on his father's left. Major Youba and other officers of the palace guard were there; Cowcroft and two junior captains of police. Hugo imagined that he had been summoned in his capacity as military adviser. If it had been a moment for amusement, he would have smiled at the thought of giving advice to people who knew so much more about fighting than he did.

"It is clear," said the ruler, "that this animal Kassim has carried out the threat which he made to Mr. Greest. He has succeeded, through influence in Lebanon, in preventing the onward passage of my arms from Beirut."

Hugo said, "The colonel's last message to me suggested that he might be able to find a way round this obstacle."

"You do not understand, Mr. Greest. Possibly a way round will be discovered. I hope so. But that is not the point. This man has dared, first, to declare his intention of opposing me. Now he has carried out his threat. If I tolerate this thing, I am no longer ruler of my own country."

There was a growl of agreement round the meeting.

"Such an action, if supported by my brother, amounts to rebellion. Rebellion must be met as soon as it raises its head. It is my intention to order that the person of Dr. Kassim be handed over to our justice. If he is not handed over, he will be taken. By force, if necessary."

War. How did one declare war? Telegrams. Ultimatums. Sir Edward Grey bowing coldly to Prince Lichnowsky. "By midnight tomorrow a state of war will exist." How long did the preliminaries take?

"We will start in five minutes' time," said the ruler. "You will travel with us, Mr. Greest. Hussein, you will remain behind at the palace, with His Excellency Sheik Fayad."

Prince Hussein seemed to have something to say about this, but was quelled by a look from his father.

"You have made the necessary arrangements, Commandant?"

Cowcroft said, "Your escort is ready, Your Highness. It will consist of twelve truckloads of police and eight lorryloads of your own guard. With a minimum force left behind to keep order in the town, this represents the total force immediately available."

"Let us hope it is sufficient to effect the arrest of one man," said the ruler with a grave smile.

It took a little more than five minutes to get going, but not a lot more. Two policemen on motorcycles headed the cavalcade, followed by two truckloads of palace guards. Then came the ruler, in his car of state, a very handsome, pale-blue, custom-built Rolls-Royce flying the royal pennant at the fore. Behind him Cowcroft, driving his own Land Rover, with Hugo in the passenger seat, and two policemen in the back. After them a cavalcade of trucks and cars bristling with armed men. Everyone looked cheerful. Hugo wondered whether this was assumed, and decided that it was not. His own feelings were mixed.

They drove south and then turned inland. The long road stretched ahead of them, straight and empty. It rose a little as they left the coast behind them, then leveled out. They had driven at a steady pace for about an hour and Hugo was wondering how much further they had to go when, rounding an outcrop of the djebel, they were suddenly in another world. It

124

was green. There were trees and bushes and cultivated fields. The tiny houses which they passed had gardens of a sort.

"If I was king of this country," said Hugo, "this is the side I'd live in."

"Not a lot in it," said Cowcroft. "They get a bit of rain in the spring. It soon dries up. I prefer the sun myself. Here's where we can look for trouble."

The road dropped sharply through a cutting in the rock. The embankment on either side was crowned with a fringe of palm trees.

"See what I mean? Ideal place for an ambush. In fact, I imagine this was the exact spot Dr. Kassim had in mind. Heavy trucks, going uphill. Wait till the first one's nearly at the top. Blow it up on a land mine. Block the far end with a couple of palms. You'd have the lot in the bag."

By the time he'd finished, they were clear of the far end of the ravine. Hugo drew a deep breath and said, "Yes, I see *just* what you mean."

"The turning ahead there leads up to the Hammuz village and fort. Seems to be some trouble."

He accelerated past the royal car, waving the driver unceremoniously to the side, stopped just short of the corner, jammed on the brakes, and jumped out.

As they rounded the corner, they could see what the trouble was. A barricade had been erected across the side road. It was nothing very elaborate. A tree trunk had been placed across the way, ballasted at each end with rocks. The motorcyclists were removing it. Major Youba was watching this being done.

Cowcroft said, "Was it guarded?"

"There were two men here." The major grinned. "When they saw us, they ran."

"In that case," said Hugo, proffering his first piece of military advice, "the quicker we move the better."

"I entirely agree," said the major.

He shouted. The tree was heaved to one side and rolled down the slope. The motorcyclists mounted. The cavalcade roared up the hill.

Any moment now, thought Hugo. What would it be? A land

mine, a hail of bullets, a mortar bomb? The uncertainty itself was curiously stimulating. What did it actually feel like to be shot? He had been wounded in play often enough; so often that he had cultivated a standard reaction to it. The slight stagger and trip, the hand clapped to the wound, always in the left shoulder or forearm, the tightening of the jaw muscles, the set of the teeth. You couldn't stop the Tiger with a bullet through his shoulder.

The palace of Sheik Hammuz was in sight ahead of them. It was almost a replica of the royal palace. There was the same deeply arched double doorway with the parapet above, the slitlike windows and crenelated battlements.

Both doors were open. The motorcyclists had dismounted and were standing one on either side. Cowcroft drove past them into the inner courtyard. He was followed by the royal car and two of the trucks in close attendance.

When they switched off their engines, they could hear the trucks and cars which were following them all grinding to a halt outside. A few words of command, muffled by the intervening walls. A moment of silence.

Then a door at the top of an interior flight of steps was thrown open and Sheik Hammuz appeared. He billowed down, seeming to bounce from step to step, and advanced upon the ruler, both hands outstretched.

"My dear brother," he said, "this is indeed an unexpected honor."

"The key word," said Cowcroft in Hugo's ear, "is 'unexpected.' I wonder what the old bastard is going to do now?"

The medium machine guns mounted in the two trucks which had entered the courtyard swiveled round casually until they were pointing in the direction of Sheik Hammuz. If he noticed them, he gave no sign.

A file of policemen marched into the courtyard and started to range themselves round it. Major Youba gestured toward a staircase. Further policemen and guards doubled toward it.

"Had I known that you were coming," said Sheik Hammuz, "I would have planned a proper reception. As it is, my poor

126

house is entirely at your command. Entirely." He looked out of the corner of his eye at the armed men who had now reached the battlement above the courtyard.

The ruler bowed abruptly and said, "The matter I have come on is urgent public business. We can discuss it out here if you wish."

"We should be more comfortable inside."

"I think so."

Sheik Hammuz turned and stood aside for the ruler to enter. Major Youba moved close at his heels. Cowcroft said, "We'd better go along, too. I'll give the orders to my men. Have you got your gun?"

Hugo nodded. He was very conscious of its weight under his left armpit.

"If any trouble starts, shoot Hammuz first and shoot him quick."

"Do you think there'll be trouble?"

"Possibly not. I fancy we've caught him with his pants down. But keep close to him. The more sure he is he'll be shot if he starts anything, the less he'll want to start."

A short passage inside the door led to a hallway. There was no evidence of air-conditioning. The fans which were turning overhead did little to lower the temperature. Half a dozen men were already seated there. Others were arriving by ones and twos. They looked, thought Hugo, like the chorus of an amateur operatic society which had been caught on the wrong foot by the unexpected raising of the curtain and were trying to slip unostentatiously into place.

The ruler and his brother were already seated. A door at the far end of the hall was flung open with a crash. An instinctive reaction sent Hugo's hand inside his coat and the butt of his gun was in his hand before he realized that the men coming in were only carrying brass pots.

When coffee had been swallowed and the cups returned, refilled, and returned again, Sheik Hammuz inclined politely toward his brother.

"You mentioned a matter of public concern?"

127

The ruler said, speaking slowly and loudly, "You will be aware that I have recently made purchases of arms and equipment for our State of Umran. My object was to fit our country to play a proper part in the affairs of the world."

"The words of an armed man are listened to with greater respect than those of one who is unarmed," agreed Sheik Hammuz.

"Some days ago, these arms reached Beirut. All arrangements had been made to bring them to Umran by air. Those arrangements have been interfered with."

Sheik Hammuz made a deprecatory movement of his hands and elbows, but said nothing.

"The man who interfered with them is living here, under your hospitality and protection. He is the Iraqi, Kassim."

A polite murmur of astonishment went up from the well-drilled chorus in the hall.

Sheik Hammuz said, "A man who could do such a thing does not deserve our hospitality. He deserves condign punishment."

Heads were nodded in grave approval.

"Since we are in agreement," said the ruler, "let the man be handed over to us, and we will ensure that his conduct receives the punishment it deserves."

"There is a difficulty," said Sheik Hammuz. "Dr. Kassim is no longer here."

A moment of silence.

"Indeed," said the ruler. "Then where is he?"

"We must suppose that he became aware that his treachery to the State of Umran was known—or might be discovered—and decided that it would be discreet to remove himself. He left last night, by car, without informing anyone of his intentions. Our guards observed him driving off in the direction of Fujaira, but had of course no authority to stop him."

The ruler considered the matter, stroking his beard thoughtfully. Then he said, "Has it occurred to you that he might have returned, as secretly as he departed? That he might, even now, be hidden somewhere in this palace?"

"It seems most unlikely."

"It is, nevertheless, possible. To assist you, I will have my men search every corner of it for you."

The ghost of a smile appeared on Sheik Hammuz's face, lingered for a moment among his billowing chins, and then dispersed.

"That would be very helpful."

The ruler barked out an order to Major Youba, who saluted and said, "The order is to search the *whole* palace."

"Yes."

"Including the women's quarters."

The ruler hesitated, and then said, "No. There will be no necessity to search the women's quarters. After all, Dr. Kassim could scarcely be there."

"I will ask Raman bin Zafra to accompany Major Youba," said Sheik Hammuz. "He will be able to point out all possible places of concealment."

He waved forward one of the men who had been standing behind his chair. Hugo thought he had never seen a more unpleasant-looking person. Hungry yellowish lidless eyes looked out from a face more gray than brown. Thin lips drew back in a smile from stained teeth, pointed like a dog's.

"It was Raman's brother, Abdullah bin Zafra," explained Sheik Hammuz, "who perpetrated the criminal folly of attacking his ruler and met a deserved fate. In fact, at your hands, Major, I believe?"

Major Youba said nothing. His hand was a few inches from his gun.

The ruler said, "As you wish. Carry out your duty, Major, and report back to me here."

"Meanwhile," said Sheik Hammuz, "allow me to offer you further refreshment."

This time, it was glasses of orange and lemon squash. Hugo took his thankfully and gulped it down. The sweat was dripping in a steady stream from his face and body.

It was a very long quarter of an hour before Major Youba returned. He said, "The man has gone."

"And it was wise of him to go," said Sheik Hammuz. "He

knew that I could not tolerate any action hostile to my brother or to our state. The arms of which you spoke were bought for the general good?"

"Certainly."

"It is your intention to use them to equip a national force, composed of *all* your loyal subjects?"

"Indeed it is. And it is my intention that you shall help and advise me in their distribution."

A faint look of uncertainty crossed Sheik Hammuz's ample features. Up to that point, thought Hugo, he had been playing a hand along lines of his own devising. For the first time, the initiative had left him. He said, "I should, of course, be very glad—"

"I was certain that you would cooperate with me," said the ruler. "And with that object, I am inviting you, my dear brother, to return with me now."

This is it, thought Hugo.

His eye photographed the exact position of every person in the crowded room. The armed policemen filling one end, the line of Sheik Hammuz's retainers along the other three walls. Cowcroft to his left, behind the ruler; Major Youba beside him; Raman bin Zafra behind Sheik Hammuz. He wondered how many hands were, at that moment, holding weapons under the all-concealing burnooses.

He had noted a substantial-looking desk to the right of the dais. It had packets of cigarettes on it and a vase of plastic flowers, and stood on a stone step. Hugo calculated that if he threw himself down, very quickly, he could get that desk and step between himself and the storm of bullets that was going to turn the room into a shambles.

This ignoble thought had scarcely registered in his mind when Sheik Hammuz rose to his feet. He said, "Nothing would give me greater pleasure, brother. I go with you very willingly." He turned to the silent lines of his people and said, "May today mark the beginning of a new era in our country. An era of cooperation and friendship."

130

Hugo drove back with Cowcroft.

"Do you think it'll work?" he said. "It all looked too easy."

"It was the speed that did it. Hammuz has got the fighting tribes behind him, all right, but it takes time to muster them."

"And then we can expect trouble?"

"I'm not sure. Carrying off Hammuz was a very shrewd move."

"They might try to rescue him?"

"If they do, they forfeit his life. They can't be under any illusions about that. And once he was gone, they wouldn't have any very obvious candidate for the throne. Did you notice a dark, thin character with a twitch sitting near Hammuz on the right?"

"My mind was on other things."

"He's Alid. A stepbrother of sorts—one of the old ruler's sons by an unofficial wife. I don't see him heading a rescue party."

"Dr. Kassim might. Do you think he really had gone?"

"If he was anywhere there, he must have been hiding under one of the beds in the women's quarters. Won't have done his image much good. Physical courage is out of fashion in England, I believe. It's still prized in these parts."

"I'll confess," said Hugo, "that if shooting had started, I was planning to fill up the hole behind that desk."

"It wouldn't have been available," said Cowcroft. "I'd have got there first."

When they arrived at the palace, the ruler, who was in high good humor, had a word with Hugo. He said, "By our morning's work we have gained ourselves a breathing space. You may now inform your colleague in Beirut that we are agreeable to extending his letter of credit for a further fourteen days. Nawaf will make all necessary arrangements with the bank."

Hussein, who still seemed depressed at not having been allowed to accompany the sortie, said, "Sayyed Nawaf is not here."

"Not here?"

"As soon as you had left the palace, he ordered his car. I understood that he caught the midday flight to Bahrain."

The ruler said, "No doubt there was business which had to be attended to. If he is not back by tomorrow, I will myself sign the order authorizing the extension."

Hugo drove back to Mohara with Cowcroft. They passed one or two patrolling cars, but the streets seemed quiet. A number of shops which had been barricaded that morning were already taking down their shutters.

"News travels fast in this neck of the woods," said Cowcroft.

When they reached police headquarters, Hugo said, "I think I ought to put a call through to London."

"Anyone in particular?"

"Taverner, at the Foreign Office. I've got his number and extension. Better make it person to person." He looked at his watch. "Two o'clock. We're three hours ahead. He should be at his desk by now."

"You're planning to tell him about this morning?" said Cowcroft thoughtfully.

"That's my idea. How long does it take to get through?"

"Depending on sandstorms and sunspots, anything from five minutes to five hours. I'll book it for you." When he came back, he was carrying a long, flimsy piece of paper in his hand. He said, "This came in yesterday evening. I forgot it in the excitement. It's about your friend."

"Which friend?"

"Colonel Delmaison. Didn't someone try to kill him in London?"

"That's right. A pair of dissatisfied customers from the Dominican Republic."

"Well, they've arrested them."

133

"Our policemen are wonderful."

"Not the British police. The Americans. They were holding them temporarily at Kennedy Airport. Some irregularity in their passports. When they got word from Scotland Yard, they made it permanent."

Hugo was looking at the telex message. Something in it was wrong. He worried at it for a moment before he realized what it was. Then he said, "Either they've got the date wrong or they've arrested the wrong men."

"Can't be the wrong men. Look at the last sentence. 'Identified by fingerprints on car.' "

Hugo started to read the message again. He said, "Then the date's wrong. The American immigration people picked them up off a flight on the evening of March twenty-third. That was a Thursday. Right?"

"I'll take your word for it."

"But the explosion was on Friday evening. That was March twenty-fourth."

"Are you sure?"

"Quite sure. I remember someone at the meeting next morning making a crack about Lady Day. That's March twenty-fifth."

"All right. They planted the stuff on the Thursday and cleared out quick. The colonel didn't happen to need his car until Friday evening."

"But," said Hugo slowly, "Colonel Rex told us that the same men had attacked him less than an hour before the explosion."

"I suppose it *was* the same men?"

"It'd be a pretty long shot if two quite different parties had been gunning for him at the same time and the same place."

"I suppose so," said Cowcroft. "Tell me the whole story. I've only heard bits of it so far."

Hugo told him the story. When he had finished, Cowcroft grunted and said, "Police messages aren't often wrong about facts. Inferences and conclusions, yes. Not things like dates and names."

"But how . . . ?"

"You say the colonel wouldn't let a doctor examine him."

134

"No. But I talked to the inspector who saw him that evening. He said there's no doubt he was hurt. He saw the blood soaking through the bandage."

"You can draw a lot of blood out of the palm of your hand with a razor blade."

"You mean he *knew* that someone had planted a bomb in his car?"

"It wouldn't be the first time someone had tried a caper like that on him, I expect. He'd take the usual precautions. Put some sort of telltale in the car. Talcum powder sprinkled on the floor, or a spot of grease on the door handle."

Hugo was thinking it out.

"Then he faked up the attack so he'd have an excuse to ask the other chap to drive his car?"

"If that's right, it looks as though you're teamed up with a pretty cold-blooded sort of sod."

"Oughtn't I to tell someone?"

"How are you going to prove it now?"

"I don't know," said Hugo unhappily.

"Anyway, I don't suppose there's a clause in your contract that lets you out if your partner turns out to be a murderer, is there?"

Hugo was saved from answering this by the telephone. The exchange said, "Your London call, Mr. Greest." And then, "I have Mr. Greest waiting for Mr. Taverner." There followed the usual interminable pause, and then Raymond Taverner's voice, as clearly as if he had been in the next room. "Greest? Good of you to call. How is everything at your end?"

Well? How *was* everything at his end?

It needed an effort of the imagination to visualize the man he was speaking to, warming his hands, perhaps, at the small fire in his grate, sniffling a little with the last cold of a dismal English spring. How could he explain to Raymond Taverner, surrounded by the solid, if faded, certainties of the British empire, that as a result of the cheese-paring tactics of the British government, he, Hugo Greest, was out on the end of a limb?

"We've had a bit of trouble here," he said.

135

"Trouble?"

Hugo did his best to explain. He said, "It seems to have blown over for the moment."

"That's fine, then."

"All the same, I think we ought to arrange to have some forces standing by. Just in case."

"What forces?"

"A couple of companies of motorized infantry would make all the difference."

"Do you suggest that I ask the Ministry of Defense to fly a half battalion of infantry to Umran?"

"I'm not suggesting anything so stupid," said Hugo. "But we've still got influence with the Oman Scouts. Couldn't it be arranged for them to pay us a visit of ceremony? The ruler would gladly invite them."

"I could suggest it, but I am very doubtful of it being agreed. We are exceedingly cautious about appearing to interfere, even indirectly, in the internal affairs of another state."

"The Americans don't think like that."

"What do you mean?"

"They've got a light cruiser standing off Umran now, ready to land a party of Marines immediately the balloon goes up."

"Are you sure of that?"

"I had it from a very reliable source."

There was an interval of silence and then Mr. Taverner said, "I don't think that would change our attitude."

"For God's sake," said Hugo, losing his temper. "Stop talking about attitudes and talk about facts. There's a valuable plum here. A bloody valuable plum. Something that could make all the difference to our balance of payments next year. Do we want it or don't we?"

"I don't think—"

"Because if we don't want it, the Americans do. They've got a trade mission here right now. And the Russians have got one coming down from Iran next week. And the Chinese have got an Iraqi agent on the spot, at least he was until he blotted his copybook and was booted out yesterday. *They* aren't sitting

136

round like a lot of desiccated old spinsters talking about attitudes—"

"I don't think," said Mr. Taverner coldly, "that we ought to
continue this discussion. Please remember you're speaking on
an open line."

The click with which he rang off added an impressive full stop
to the sentence.

"Nice work," said Cowcroft. "I loved 'desiccated old spinsters.' Not that it'll do a mite of good. I've been dealing with the
Foreign Office for thirty years. You've as much chance of getting a positive decision out of them nowadays as you have of
cutting your hair with a motor mower. They don't recognize
concrete problems any longer. Awkward sordid things, I mean,
like men and money. They think in terms of attitudes and
aspects and tendencies." He paused, and added unexpectedly,
"It's the same thing with critics. Had you noticed? When they
get old and tired, they don't bother to read the book they're
meant to be criticizing. They hang it onto a convenient ten-
dency. It's less trouble."

Hugo was only half attending. The other half was revising his
opinion of Martin Cowcroft. It was interesting to discover a real
mind behind that leathery façade.

"Is that right about the Russians?"

"I got it from Nawaf. He says one of their deputy trade minis-
ters is coming on here next week from Teheran."

"I hope it keeps fine for him," said Cowcroft. "Where *is*
Nawaf? There's a rumor he cleared out when the trouble
started."

"The ruler didn't seem to know that he'd gone. If he has
bunked, it'd mean he was in with Dr. Kassim. Funny. He didn't
seem that sort of person at all."

"Arabs are like that," said Cowcroft. "You can never tell what
sort of people they are until it's too late to do anything about
it. Come down and get some grub at the police canteen. I think
we've earned it."

Hugo slept well that night. The next morning after breakfast,
he walked down to the jetty. There were one or two purchases

he still had to make for his housewarming party. He told himself that it was a matter of duty to get to know Bob Ringbolt better. That was the reason for the party. "And if he brings Tammy with him, I'll be very glad to see her, too," he said to himself. "She's a nice girl."

Moharram was taking down his shutters. Hugo said, "I noticed you were shut yesterday, Mo. Why was that?"

Moharram grinned and said, "Yesterday I went out fishing."

"You're a bloody liar. But if that's your story, you stick to it. I want some olives and a jar of salted peanuts. And some packets of crisps. Have you got a boat?"

"A boat?"

"You said you went out fishing."

"Boats, you get them at the dhow harbor. Nice boats. They let you have one for the day or the week."

"A day would do."

"I fix it for you. When you want him?"

"Her."

"You want a girl, too?"

"No, no. Boats are female. We say 'her.'"

"Boats are like wives," said Moharram. "They're bloody awkward to handle when the wind gets up. I've got four wives. None of them any bloody use now."

"I want her tomorrow. I'm going over to look at the Ducks."

"Nothing to see there. Just sand."

"I'm fond of sand," said Hugo. "Let's have a few of those stick sausages as well."

He spent the morning in the office, half expecting a message from London but hearing nothing. He had no doubt that the ponderous machinery in Whitehall was grinding round, the attitude of the Afro-Asian block at UNO being predicted, the views of the opposition appreciated, the reactions in twenty different countries considered, if two companies of the Oman Scouts paid a courtesy visit to a neighbor in that remote corner of the Gulf.

At midday, a messenger arrived from the ruler. He had a note authorizing the extension of the Beirut credit for a further

138

fourteen days. Since the ruler had signed it himself, Hugo gathered that Nawaf had not reappeared. He made the necessary arrangements to inform the Arab Bank in Beirut, and sent a cable to Colonel Rex at the Hotel Continentale, giving him the good news.

After that, he went home for lunch and took his afternoon siesta. He found himself slipping back easily into the routine which he had abandoned, as he thought forever, fifteen years before.

At five o'clock, he had a shower and several cups of scalding sugarless tea. Then he strolled across to the next building and knocked on the door of Ringbolt's flat.

He could hear voices inside, but it was a few moments before the door was opened. Closing down the wireless transmitter, thought Hugo. It was Bob himself, looking cool and neat in white shirt and shorts, with sandals on his bare feet.

He said, "Come along in, Hugo. We've got a compatriot of yours here."

Charlie Wandyke was sharing a sofa with Tammy. He had a large glass of beer in his hand and looked happy. He said, "I hear you've been on the warpath, Hugo." Tammy said, "The Tiger goes to war," looked devoutly at him, and spoiled the effect by grinning. "I bet it was fun. Roaring along the road with your guns out. Storming the desert fortress. Beau Geste rides again."

"It wasn't like that at all," said Hugo.

"We've heard all sorts of stories. Is it true you volunteered to head the search of the harem?"

"Certainly not."

"Tell, tell. What *did* you do?"

"Give the man a chance," said Ringbolt. "He hasn't got a drink yet. What'll it be?"

"Beer, please," said Hugo. "And I didn't do anything, except keep one eye open for a place to duck into when the bullets started flying. Only they didn't."

"No bullets?"

"Not one. We went, we saw, we conquered. And we came back with the booty. One sheik, discomposed but undamaged."

"It was a smart move, that," said Ringbolt. "With their king in balk, there aren't a lot of gambits left to them. There's some sort of cousin, I believe, but he's no great shakes, by all accounts."

"According to my foreman," said Wandyke, "—and I've never known him to be wrong about anything yet—Dr. Kassim hasn't gone. He may not have been in the palace, but he was hiding out somewhere. As long as he's there, I shouldn't count on a walkover. I've been hearing stories about that boy."

"You think he's dangerous?"

"I think he's poison. Until I've seen his hide nailed up on the wall, I'm not taking any chances myself."

"What are you going to do, Charlie?" said Ringbolt. "You can't pack the mine up and take it away in your pocket."

"No. But I can immobilize the machinery and move everyone out. We had a practice evacuation yesterday. We did it in half an hour. And I bet you we'd halve that time if we had a crowd of wuzzies with knives up our backsides."

"You've got your boat, then," said Hugo. His beer suddenly seemed to have lost some of its flavor. He thought Charlie probably knew what he was talking about.

"A thirty-foot diesel-engined dhow, with all modern conveniences."

"It sounds just the job," said Hugo. "And what arrangements are you making for getting your party out, Bob?"

This was something which could have been said in a lot of different ways. Hugo's tone was fairly neutral, but it produced a moment of silence. Then Ringbolt said, "We shall be all right, Hugo. I guess you saw our wireless installation the other night. I've got Birnie on the set right now. He's been talking to our fleet commander. He'll send in a couple of helicopters if we want them."

"And if trouble starts, you'll send for them?"

The silence this time was more marked. Then Ringbolt said equably, "All right, Hugo. I know what you're thinking. I'm not making excuses. Right now I'm acting under orders. Our State Department has got some pretty rigid ideas about a situation of

140

this sort. There's two ways of tackling it. You can stay put until the local inhabitants simply have to chop you. Then, when everyone's steamed up about it, your real forces move in and knock hell out of the local opposition, and rely on everyone saying, 'Serve the bastards right.' That's what you did with your General Gordon in Khartoum, right?"

"As far as I can remember, it took us about ten years to move in on the Mahdi. But that was roughly the principle, I agree."

"Things move faster nowadays. World opinion's more mobilized. If we put the Marines ashore in Umran without a mighty good excuse, the doves would be raising hell in the United Nations within twenty-four hours. They might even suggest we were out to collar the smitherite concession by force."

"They'd be wrong, of course," said Wandyke with a grin.

"You said *two* ways," said Hugo.

"That's right. Well, the preferred way nowadays is what you might call the dustpan and brush method. You keep well clear until the local factions have finished cutting each other's throats, and then you arrive and sweep up the mess. You pat the winner on the back and tell him you've been backing him all along and you've come in to help him restore the economy of his ravaged country. The Marines arrive, same as in method A, but this time they're not aiming to fight anyone. They're there to see no one loots the essential supplies you're bringing in, or rapes the Red Cross nurses."

"But the end result's the same?"

"Right. Only you get patted on the back for being humanitarian instead of being kicked in the crotch for a colonialist pig."

"Well, thanks for explaining it."

"I should have made it clear, Hugo, that there's a seat in the helicopter for you."

Hugo hesitated. It was not that he was in any doubt as to his answer. He wanted to phrase it without sounding pompous. In the end he said, "I'm not really a free agent in the matter, Bob. Under my contract with the ruler, I think I have to give him three months' notice."

He caught a fleeting glimpse of the smile on Tammy's face

141

and saw her lips frame "Hold that Tiger." He added, quickly, "Anyway, if worse comes to the worst, I've got a boat, too. It's not a very big one. I was planning to take it over to the Ducks tomorrow. I take it Friday's a holiday for you as well."

"That's right," said Ringbolt. There was a faint look of puzzlement on his face.

"I only asked because I didn't want to rob you of your secretary if it was a working day. Would you care to come along, Tammy?"

Tammy said, without the least hesitation, "I most certainly would." And added, "Grrr, grrr, grrr-rh."

Chapter 17 / Beirut: Wednesday and Thursday

Wednesday in Beirut brought up one of the sudden storms that sweep in from the eastern end of the Mediterranean, smash against the mountains, and disappear into the desert, leaving behind a litter of torn sun blinds, shredded travel posters, and a general feeling of freshness and well-being.

Colonel Rex spent the morning in his room at the Hotel Continentale with Mr. Sharif, working through packing arrangements. He said, "It's absolute nonsense to think of *flying in* the trucks or the crated helicopters. With the small freight planes we're using, you'd need one plane for each truck. If we were able to charter one of the American maxi-transporters, we could get several trucks on each. But they couldn't land on the runway at Mohara."

Sharif nodded. He had come to the same conclusion. He said, "The trucks will have to go by sea. Your client will not object. What he needs now are guns, not trucks."

"Right. So we put all the small arms, automatic weapons, mortars, ammunition, and perhaps one pack howitzer on the first plane. The rest of the howitzers and the signaling and engineers' stores on the second. The four remaining planes can take the light A.A., the antitank guns, and anything else which is left. When will the first plane leave?"

"Tonight."

"How is Hafiz fixing it?"

"The loading will be done in a spare bay at the far end of the terminal buildings. It is the old pilgrim compound. The stuff will be taken from the transit warehouse, by trucks, as soon as it is dusk. It will cost a great deal of money to organize, but he has a reliable foreman whose gang will do what they are told. They are all of them his sons and cousins."

"And the warehouse will release the cargo?"

"Naturally, they will have an official order to do so. Hafiz has studied the regulations of the Israeli boycott. There is nothing to prevent goods being transported onwards as long as they remain in a state which itself subscribes to the boycott arrangements."

"Which Bahrain does?"

"Most certainly."

"And when they are there?"

"Equally, there will be no reason why they should not be sent forward to Umran. Umran is also a party to the boycott."

"Something tells me that the second leg will need a certain amount of fixing."

"I understand that a high official from Umran is already in Bahrain to expedite matters."

"Good," said the colonel. He had, in the course of a long life, arranged for the transport of many different cargoes by many different routes. By road, by rail, by air, and by sea. By pack mule, by camel, by barge, and by canoe. Even, on one occasion, by aerial ropeway to the top of a mountain and down the other side by sledge. He had invariably found that the lubricant which eased the wheels around was money; money disbursed to the right person in the right amounts at the right time. It seemed to be working here. Hafiz clearly knew his job and was earning the very large sum which the colonel had paid him. And which the colonel, in turn, had borrowed, at much risk, from the Jannis.

Colonel Rex was reminded of his obligations by a telephone call which arrived while he was eating his lunch. It summoned him to a meeting that afternoon at the office of the Jannis' lawyer. The colonel protested, but was overruled so sharply that he said no more. He finished his meal and, unusually, ordered a large brandy. The drink did something to dispel a

144

cold feeling in the pit of his stomach. His instincts, which hardly ever deceived him, told him that he was running into trouble.

When he arrived, there were two men in the lawyer's office. The Janni he had dealt with and an older, thicker, swarthier version of him whom the colonel took to be his brother. The lawyer was not in evidence.

The younger Janni said, "We hear that you have concluded arrangements to dispatch a first planeload of rifles and automatic weapons to Bahrain this evening."

"And mortars," said the brother.

"Is this true?"

"Perfectly true."

"Then your security has been very bad."

"What do you mean?"

"If *we* have heard about it, do you suppose that half Beirut does not know about it, too? That the minister will not soon know?"

"I hope that his intelligence service will be less well informed than yours."

"It may be so. It may not. It brings me to what I had to say. Your letter of credit with the Arab Bank is encashable in series? That is right? It would be the usual arrangement."

"It is encashable in multiples of five hundred pounds against bills of lading and invoices of that amount."

"As I supposed. When you produce the airway bills covering the first planeload, the bank will release to you—how much?"

The colonel affected to make a calculation. In fact, he knew the answer. He had worked it out that morning. His hesitation was to cover a more difficult computation. How accurately would the Jannis be able to compute the value of an individual consignment of weapons? He dared not pitch it too low. They were already suspicious. On the other hand, if he named the real figure, he knew exactly what to expect.

He said, "If the cargo is loaded in accordance with our provisional schedule—"

"Is there some doubt about it?"

145

"We are very close to the safety weight limit. It might be necessary to leave some of the mortar ammunition behind."

"A pity," said the elder brother. He seemed to have a fixation about mortars.

"On the basis of the full scheduled load, I would hope to encash fifty thousand pounds."

The younger Janni looked at some papers on the desk in front of him and said, "By my calculation it should be nearer seventy thousand."

"Does it matter?" said the colonel smoothly. "When I go to the bank, we shall be able to calculate exactly what the figure is. If the cargo we dispatch tonight is a little less valuable, we shall make it up on subsequent deliveries."

"I am not interested in subsequent deliveries. I intend that my twenty percent share of the total profit shall be paid to me from the proceeds of the first dispatch."

There was a moment of silence. Then the colonel said mildly, "I don't think I can agree to that, you know. We are in this business on a partnership basis. We divide the profit in the agreed proportions, as it becomes available."

"I can see that you do not understand the situation. You are engaged in the purchase and sale of arms. You have the necessary licenses, of course. It is a legitimate business enterprise. Nevertheless, I can assure you that if I were to speak a word in the right quarter, none of those arms, no single gun, no single round of ammunition, would leave the airport warehouses tonight or any other night for some time to come."

"But would that be a sensible thing to do? We would both be losers. I would lose my share of the profits. You would lose yours, and your loan would be in jeopardy."

The younger Janni smiled. He said, "You have not thought this thing through, Colonel. Were such a contingency to arise, and I hope it will not, the entire consignment would, after a suitable interval, be offered at auction. I should buy it. Naturally, since it will be a forced sale, it will be at a depreciated price. And there is a ready market for armaments in this part of the world. Certain items in particular."

146

His brother appeared to shape, with his mouth, the word "mortars."

Colonel Rex took a taxi back to the hotel. The storm was already passing. The gusts of wind were capricious rather than fierce. The colonel tipped the driver extravagantly and ran up the steps of the hotel, ignoring the umbrella which the porter held out.

Since he was fairly certain that he would now be watched, he made a point of behaving as naturally as possible. He visited the barbershop in the hotel and had a haircut, shampoo, and scalp massage. He would have liked a facial massage as well, but there was a weakness in his jawbone which made such a procedure dangerous except in the most expert hands. Then he went back to his room, removed most of his clothes, turned up the air-conditioning, lay down on his bed, and made a conscious effort to relax. The realization had been creeping up on him for some time that he was getting too old for his chosen profession. He knew more than one man who had failed to get out at the right time, had stayed until he was mentally as well as financially hooked, had finished, if he was lucky enough to survive, in a back-street pension, a garrulous cadging wreck. This was the moment of decision. All that he had to do was to get his hands on the money due on the first consignment. The Jannis had been very close in their estimate. It was £68,500. He had a furnished villa outside Cairo, taken in another name. Only a few people in the Egyptian Ministry of Defense knew his real name and calling. He had performed useful services for them in the past and they would certainly secure him the necessary documents and permits to enable him to stay permanently. The little lady who looked after the villa for him was an agreeable if unexciting bed companion. Perhaps he would marry her and settle down.

So thinking, he drifted into sleep. It was nearly eight o'clock when he woke. The evening, as so often after a day of storm, was quite perfect. The air was fresh and all the stars were out. He dressed carefully and took a taxi to the casino, where he dined. After dinner, he watched the first of the two nightly shows and got back to the hotel just before midnight. The desk clerk handed him an envelope.

The colonel collected his keys and walked up to his room. There he turned on the bedside light and examined the envelope. It had been clumsily opened and resealed. The note said, "Number one safely away." It was unsigned.

The colonel stuffed the note and envelope into his pocket, turned out the lights, let himself out into the passage, and relocked the room door from the outside. The kitchen quarters were quiet and deserted. The colonel unlocked the back door, using his own key. He had borrowed this key from the manager when he had confirmed the booking of his room. The manager had not appeared to find anything strange in the request. Twenty years of looking after a hotel in Beirut had hardened him to human vagaries. There had been the sheik who had kept one of his wives in a cabin trunk and another who kept a crocodile in his bath. Compared with these, a guest who paid for an expensive suite and appeared unwilling to sleep in it was a minor mystery.

The colonel took a careful look up and down the alleyway and then crossed it, walking briskly, and plunged into the complex of tiny streets beyond it. Every now and then he stopped. The complete silence assured him that he was not being followed. In ten minutes he was at his lodging, and in another ten was in bed. Fara was both sympathetic and intelligent. She saw that he had had a trying day. She therefore refrained from speech and comforted him with her body.

The colonel woke early. By half-past six he was up and dressed. There was much to do. While Fara made him a cup of coffee, he used the telephone. A sleepy Mr. Sharif answered him. From a muttered feminine protest which came to him over the wire, the colonel guessed that he had caught him in bed. He said, "Wake up and listen to me. This is important. You'd better write it down."

"Wait a moment." There followed the sound of a slap on bare flesh, a squeal, and Mr. Sharif said, "O.K., Colonel."

148

"You have the airway bills, certified by the captain of the airplane?"

"Yes."

"And the invoices?"

"Right here."

"Have you confirmed the total?"

"In sterling, sixty-seven thousand, one hundred and fifty pounds. In Lebanese currency—"

"Never mind about Lebanese currency. Why are we more than a thousand short?"

"Some of the mortars and mortar ammunition had to be left behind to make room for the pack howitzer."

The colonel said, "I see." It occurred to him that Sharif might have done a private deal with the pilot of the aircraft and arranged to split the difference with him. The idea did not displease him. If people cheated in small matters, it made them easier to deal with in big ones. He said, "Now listen. Take all the documents to the Arab Bank. If you telephone the manager and explain your business, you will be allowed into the bank before it opens for public business at ten o'clock. There is a side door for private customers and staff. They will admit you at nine o'clock. Ask for the money to be ready in dollar bills. Specify the larger denominations. Five-hundred- and thousand-dollar bills will be best. You can pack such an amount easily into a brief-case. When you leave the bank, also by the side door, turn to the left. This will bring you out into Mustaq Road. Immediately opposite the back of the bank there is a large café."

"I know it."

"Good. I will meet you there at half-past nine. There is a room at the back where we shall be able to do business in private."

The colonel's next call was to the air terminal. He found that there were two scheduled flights daily for Cairo. There was an MEA Viscount which left at ten forty-five in the morning; a Lufthansa VC-10 at seven o'clock in the evening. The booking clerk confirmed that neither plane was likely to be full. If he was at the airport thirty minutes before departure time, he could guarantee him a seat.

149

The colonel was back in his room at the hotel by half-past seven, telephoning room service for his breakfast. The boy who brought it up found him shaving.

At nine o'clock he left the hotel on foot and walked slowly down the street. He had no difficulty in spotting the young man in the blue serge suit who detached himself from the shop door opposite and started to stroll after him.

The colonel smiled to himself. What had to be done next demanded finesse, since to be effective it had to appear to be accidental. He had to wait for nearly a quarter of an hour before circumstances were propitious. The street ahead was reasonably empty, and a single taxi was coming up behind him. The colonel allowed the taxi to draw level with him, then stopped it with a wave of his arm, jumped in, and said, "To the station, and make it fast." The taxi driver needed no second bidding. Making things fast was one of the minor pleasures of his life. He was going at fifty kilometers an hour before he was out of third gear. The colonel risked a quick glance back. The youth in the blue suit was looking wildly about him for a second taxi, but having no luck.

At the station, the colonel paid off the taxi, walked in at one end of the waiting room and out at the other. He was waiting in the back room of the café when Sharif arrived. The time, he noted, was twenty minutes to ten. From the smile on Sharif's face he gathered that all had gone well.

"No trouble at all." Sharif opened the smart black briefcase and started to unpack the neat bundles of dollar bills.

"My dear fellow," said the colonel, "leave them where they are." He detached five thousand-dollar bills and handed them to Sharif. "The laborer is worthy of his hire." He took out a further bill, this time of five hundred dollars, and said, "I will buy the briefcase from you as well. Right?"

"That is very generous," said Sharif. "You will be glad to know that I have already spoken to our friend Hafiz. The dispatch last night went so smoothly that he has every confidence that tonight's should go equally well."

"I am glad to hear it," said the colonel. His mind was working

150

with the exceptional speed and clarity which it exhibited in moments of crisis. He had found that danger, deliberately courted, pumped adrenaline into his mental as well as his physical processes.

It had been his plan to leave that evening with the proceeds of the previous night's dispatch. Dare he now try to double his money? The first operation had gone so smoothly that the temptation was overpowering. He calculated times, distances, and probabilities, and arrived at an answer so quickly that there was scarcely a break in the conversation. He said, "Then let us follow the same program tomorrow." Glancing at his watch, he added, "Exactly the same program." The time was five to ten. A taxi would get him to the airport in twenty minutes. There were risks, certainly. But for an additional seventy thousand pounds, risks were acceptable.

When he left the café, he made his way back on foot to his lodging. Fara was out and the flat was empty. After some thought, he put the briefcase on a high shelf in the kitchen and positioned three saucepans in front of it. He had often found that simple hiding places were the best. Then he walked back to the hotel, entered it openly, and stationed himself in the lounge with a *café filtre* and a copy of *Free Lebanon*, one of the racier Beirut newspapers.

The telephone call which he was expecting came at shortly after eleven o'clock. It was young Janni and his voice was harsh with suspicion. He said, "Have you seen the bank yet?"

"No," said the colonel, equally sharply. "Why should I?"

There was a pause at the other end. The counterattack was unexpected.

"We had imagined that you would have presented the airway bills covering the first dispatch, which we understood went off on time—"

"Certainly."

"And received the appropriate money."

"I'm afraid you know very little of how these matters are arranged," said the colonel. He was still speaking without any hint of apology. "The airway bills have to be certified by the

151

airline office, which, incidentally, does not start work until half-past ten. I have arranged to collect them at four o'clock this afternoon, when they will be handed to me personally and to no one else. I have also arranged to attend at the Arab Bank and encash them at half-past ten tomorrow. If you wish to be present, I shall have no objection."

There was a long pause. The colonel imagined that young Janni must be consulting his brother. He himself was relying on the fact that neither of them would have had much practical experience of the air-freighting of goods. In the end, young Janni said mildly, "Very well, Colonel Delmaison. We will meet at the bank at half-past ten tomorrow." There was a pause, then he added, "Might I give you some advice? If I were you, I should not go very far from your hotel today."

The colonel replaced the receiver thoughtfully. He would have preferred threats to such studied politeness.

After lunch, he approached the reception clerk and said, "Will you please prepare my bill. I shall be using my room for one further night, but shall not be dining at the hotel this evening. I may have to leave very early tomorrow morning, and should like to discharge my account now."

When the bill came, the colonel paid it, in dollars, and added a very handsome sum, "To cover contingencies." When the clerk came back with the receipted bill, he conveyed to the colonel the compliments of the manager and the hope that he had enjoyed his stay. The colonel said that he had enjoyed it very much. He proposed now to take a siesta in his room, and would the exchange please be told to put through no calls until six o'clock.

The reception clerk assured the colonel that he would attend to this personally, and was further rewarded. Ten minutes later, the colonel was asleep. One of his most formidable attainments was an ability to relax in times of stress.

The telephone woke him. He looked at his watch. It was five o'clock. The receptionist was most apologetic. If the caller had not assured him that it was of the utmost urgency—

"All right, all right," said the colonel. "I'm awake now. Put him through."

It was Sharif, and his voice was thin with fear. He said, "This afternoon, at three o'clock—"

"Speak more slowly. What happened at three o'clock?"

"Hafiz was killed. A car ran him down. It failed to stop. The police—"

"Never mind about the police. Was it an accident?"

"I do not think so."

"All right. Now we know." The colonel considered the matter coldly. "We shall have to revise our plans. Come to the hotel at seven o'clock. You may come quite openly. By then I shall have made the necessary arrangements."

By then he would have made the necessary arrangements. By then he should be on the evening plane to Cairo.

Against just such an emergency, he kept, in a cleverly constructed pocket in his suitcase, a second passport. It was in the name of D. E. Martin, and a few simple alterations in his appearance—a toupé covering his bald patch, a touch of matching color in his hair, and a pair of heavy gold-rimmed glasses—transformed him into a sufficient likeness of the serious middle-aged man in the passport photograph.

In the time available to them, the opposition would not have been able to mount any very thorough blocking operation at the airport. He had little doubt that the innocuous Mr. Martin would pass.

The only question was whether he could get clear of the hotel. The front would certainly be watched. Would they trouble about the back? There was only one way of finding out.

A glance out of the kitchen door was enough. The young man whom he had evaded that morning was standing on the other side of the alley, apparently admiring the pointed toes of his own shoes. The colonel, who was wearing rubber soles, crossed the alley in six quick and silent steps. The youth looked up, and started, much too late, to take his hands out of his pockets. The colonel hit him a swinging backhand blow on the side of the neck and, as his body came forward, jerked a knee up into his face.

By the time the youth, spitting blood, teeth, and obscenities, had got onto his knees, the colonel was three streets away, and

153

walking fast. Speed, at this point, was more important than secrecy. The changes to be made in his appearance, though trivial, had to be made carefully, and took time. To be certain of a seat on the plane, he ought to be at the airport soon after six. It was now twenty past five. Enough time, but by no means too much.

As he let himself into the house and climbed the stairs to Fara's apartment, he ran over in his mind the plans he had made, the contingencies he had to watch for, the unexpected elements of bad luck which complicated the most perfectly conceived schemes and had to be met by improvisation.

The door was locked and he assumed therefore that Fara was out. He was fumbling for his key when she heard him and shouted, "All right. I'm coming."

She opened the door, and stood there for a moment as he stepped forward to kiss her. The look in her eyes told him the truth, but much too late. The man who had been standing behind the door with a knife had never had an easier mark.

When Sharif arrived at the hotel at seven o'clock, the receptionist was unable to help him. The colonel had paid his bill and vacated his room. He had left no forwarding address. (It is a fact that at the precise moment that he said these words, the colonel's body was being carefully sewn up in a long sack, the bottom half of which was full of dry cement. As soon as it was dark, a motorboat would tow the sack a mile out to sea and the towrope would be cut.)

"If you should be able to contact Colonel Delmaison," said the receptionist, "perhaps you could tell him that we hold a cable for him, from Umran. It was delivered five minutes after he left. It is marked 'Urgent.' "

154

Chapter 18 / *Coitus Interruptus*

"It'd be nothing more than he deserves," said Tammy, "if you refused to have anything more to do with him."

"I'm afraid I'm stuck with him," said Hugo.

"He's a murderer."

"Not proved."

"It's obvious. He knew they'd put a bomb in his car and he faked things so that poor little Urban walked into it."

"I didn't know you knew Mr. Nussbaum."

"I'd met him. He wanted to make himself known to Bob. Arms salesmen always keep in with the State Department. I thought he was a nice little man. He told me all about his wife and children."

"Watch the fish. It's going to fall off that stick in a moment."

It was a very small shark. They had caught it on their way over to the island. With its scrawny neck, its bulging stomach, and its sad eyes, it looked like an advertisement for Oxfam.

Tammy had constructed the fire out of driftwood, showing remarkable expertise.

"I learned to do this sort of thing at summer camp," she said. "It's an American institution. Any parents who can afford it shoot their children off to one at the beginning of the long vacation. It does both parties good, I guess. It gets the children out of their parents' hair for a while and teaches them how to get along with other people. For the first twenty-four hours you were homesick, then you met some marvelous boy. . . ."

She sighed and rotated the small shark. She had spitted it on a long stick, balanced between two uprights. It was beginning to go brown at the edges.

"Some marvelous boy?"

"His name was Homer. I was ten and he was fourteen. I thought he was the most perfect thing I'd ever seen. Like a young god or something." She sighed again. "I met him last year. He's in an office on Wall Street, and he'd already begun to get *fat*. Would you believe it?"

"I expect there were others."

"Certainly." She looked at him out of the corner of her cat's eyes. "The first time I was actually *seduced* was on my fifteenth birthday."

"I'm surprised it didn't happen before."

"It was meant to make you feel grown up. It just made me feel messy."

"Watch it," said Hugo. The fish had canted dangerously.

"Tell me something," said Tammy when the fish had been rescued. "What are you aiming to get out of this?"

"Out of what?" Hugo's mind was entirely on her.

"Out of coming out here. You had a lovely job, plenty of money, and a lot of lovely girls to play around with. . . ."

"The lovely job had finished. I had a bit of money, but certainly not enough to keep me warm for the rest of my life. And as for the lovely girls, if you think it's fun making love to a girl with four cameras, two sound booms, and a studio full of extras leering at you, then think again."

"O.K. I'll give you that. But why Umran?"

"It's a job. Come to that, why are you here?"

"It's a job."

"Not a very suitable job for a girl, I should have thought."

"That's where you're wrong. What you see here is no ordinary girl. It's a dedicated, case-hardened agent of the U.S. State Department. And anyway, there are jobs girls can do and men can't."

"Such as?"

"Such as, for instance, if Prince Hussein should wish for a consort. I'd be right in line for the situation. It's been suggested in certain quarters already."

156

Hugo sat bolt upright and said, in tones of outrage, " *Who* has suggested it?"

"The young man hinted at it. He implied that his father would not be averse."

"And Bob would let you do it?"

"If it cemented the entente, he would surely regard it as my dooty."

Hugo lay back again. He said, "I thought for a moment you were serious."

Tammy said nothing. She had buried both of her small, square feet in the sand and was twiddling them round until the tops of her toes appeared like little pink and white sea creatures coming up for air. Finally she said, "Tell me something, Hugo. If there really was trouble and we cleared out by kind permission of the officer commanding United States battle cruiser *Archimandrite*, would you come along?"

"I'd like to, but I don't really see how I could."

"Bad for the Tiger image?"

"Don't talk rubbish."

"What then? British phlegm? The stiff upper lip? 'I say, old man, do you think those wuzzies are going to attack us?' 'Can't, old boy. It's the fourth of June. Everyone knows the fourth of June's a holiday.' "

"That sort of thing went out thirty years ago."

"There must be a little of it left," said Tammy wistfully. "In odd holes and corners. Don't tell me the last pair of spats has been laid away in mothballs, the last monocle broken."

"If you want to hear the true voice of Britain," said Hugo, rolling over onto his stomach and reaching for his discarded jacket, "I will read you the text of a message received at eighteen hundred hours last night. It is marked 'Top Secret,' so I am committing a serious offense against the Official Secrets Act by revealing the contents to you. No matter." He adjusted an imaginary monocle in his right eye and read out: " 'Your telephonic communication timed fourteen thirty hours local time on April 26 and your request transmitted in that message now considered by all relevant authorities here. Stop. Concluded that on balance of politico-diplomatic considerations and taking account all factors transmitted you verbally by department Foreign Office concerned not presently desirable initiate or suggest any visit armed forces from your southern neighbors to you. Stop. Should situation change will inform you forthwith.' "

"What does it mean?"

"It means no. It took them seventy expensive words to say it, but it means no."

"I can't make out that last bit at all about them telling you if the situation changed. You'd know about that before they did, I should think."

"I agree. Palmerston would have sent a gunboat. Or a message saying, 'Not bloody likely, chum. You stick it out.' Now we have to put in slush about relevant departments and politico-diplomatic considerations."

"It's not just you," said Tammy. "We all do it. The U.S. State Department is just as bad. Worse, I guess. They'd have taken a hundred words to say it, and put in something about the man on the spot exercising independent judgment, and a prayer for the United Nations. That would be to cover them, if things went badly wrong."

"I bet the Russians don't behave like that."

"The Russians! My goodness, have you ever seen one of their messages? They'd have been twice as long again. They're *terrified* of saying anything which isn't authorized in writing by some superior authority."

"Have you ever seen a Russian message?"

Tammy looked a shade embarrassed, and said, "Once or twice. In the line of duty. What I really wanted to say was that you mustn't think too badly of Bob. He has to keep in wireless touch, through the Navy, with his bosses in Washington. He really is tied by the leg."

"Did I sound as though I was thinking badly of him yesterday evening?"

"I was waiting for you to insert your fingers in the top pocket of your vest, extract a white feather, and hand it to him."

"He could have handed it right back," said Hugo. "I'm a terrific coward. Do you think that fish is ready?"

"I guess it's as ready as it's ever going to be." Tammy

removed the stick and tilted the incinerated lumps of shark onto two cardboard plates which they had brought with them. They tasted surprisingly good. The rest of the meal was tuna fish sandwiches made with unleavened bread, apples, and a bottle of red wine bought from Moharram. It was labeled "Jolly-grape —guaranteed produce of many leading French vineyards."

After the meal, Hugo buried the bottle and the debris and said, "I'm going to sleep," and in a few minutes was asleep. Tammy propped herself up on one elbow and took a long and thoughtful look at him. He slept easily, on his right side. His face was a bit red, but he was not sweating or snoring.

When Hugo woke up, he rolled over, saw the remains of the fire, remembered where he was, and sat up. There was no sign of Tammy. Then he saw her red head bobbing in the water fifty yards out to sea. She swam leisurely toward him and got to her feet as the ground shelved toward the island. He then saw that she was naked.

She said, "I couldn't put on a bathing suit. The water's heaven. Just the right temperature, and like it was full of bath salts." She added politely, "I hope you don't mind."

"Not a scrap."

She spread a towel in the dip in the sand, disposed herself on it, and said, "Now that you have seen all of me, there's not much point in covering anything up, is there?"

"None at all," said Hugo. He started to take off the cotton undershirt which, with a pair of shorts, was all he was wearing at that moment.

"Were you planning to have a swim?"

"I had more immediate plans," said Hugo thickly.

"Involving me?"

"Involving you."

"Well, all right. Only one request from this girl. Do every-thing terribly slowly. I've always found that the prologue is better than the play."

"All right," said Hugo. He wished he could have sounded as cool and sophisticated about it as she did.

It was at this precise moment that they heard, muffled by the distance but horribly distinct, the boom of a gun.

Part Three / Infighting

Chapter 19 / Trouble

"My God," said Tammy. "What was that?"

"Trouble," said Hugo. He was putting on his undershirt. "That was from the ruler's palace. It sounded like that big gun in the courtyard blasting off. I thought it was strictly for ornament. I must have been wrong."

"What's happening? What does it mean?" She, too, was scrambling back into her clothes.

"That's what we've got to find out."

While they were on the island, the tide had come in and the boat, which they had beached, was now afloat in two feet of water. They tumbled aboard. Hugo pulled up the anchor and started the engine.

"What are you aiming to do?"

"First stop, the flats," said Hugo. "Find out what the form is and take it from there."

"Do you think something really has started? They might just have fired that piece off for fun."

"Listen," said Hugo. He slowed the engine, and as the boat slid quietly forward through the water, they could hear, muted by the distance but quite clear, the rattle of musketry.

"Fires, too," said Hugo. From several places in the town columns of smoke were going up into the still evening air.

A sparkle of flashes showed from the shadows at the end of the dhow quay.

"I wonder what they're shooting at," said Tammy.

"Us," said Hugo, and heaved the boat round in a violent half circle.

"Were they really?"

"They certainly were."

As he said it, something hit the stern of the boat with a rap and whined off out to sea.

"Wow," said Tammy. "Do you think we ought to lie down or something?"

"They're not likely to hit us now," said Hugo. "It was an incredibly lucky shot at that." They were a quarter of a mile from the shore.

"What next?"

Hugo was looking at the fuel gauge. He said, "If we had enough fuel, I'd have run you straight across to the coast of Iran and put you ashore; only we haven't."

"*Put* me ashore?" said Tammy thoughtfully. "Just what were you planning to do yourself?"

"I think I ought to get back and see what's happening. After all, I am the ruler's military adviser. It looks to me as though he might be able to use some military advice right now."

"It certainly sounds like it."

"We'll go back to the island and lie up on the other side, out of sight. If anyone's bothering about us, they'll assume that we've gone straight on. It'll be dark in two hours. I ought to be able to find somewhere to land, up the coast, closer to the palace."

"What then?"

"It's impossible to make any sort of plan until I find out what's happening."

"And where am I while you're finding out?"

"Sitting on the island, twiddling your toes."

"That I most certainly am not. Do you know what happens on these sandbanks after dark? Big crabs, big as soup plates, come creeping out of their holes. Thousands of them, clicking their claws. Anything they find there, they eat. *Anything.*"

"How do you know?"

"I read it in a book."

"I think it's nonsense."

"It may be nonsense, but I'm not aiming to find out."

164

"All right," said Hugo. "You can come with me. But you've got to do what you're told."

"I've always been a submissive sort of girl," said Tammy.

It was nine o'clock by Hugo's watch when they finally beached the boat on the shores of Umran. The moon, which was almost full, was not due to rise for another hour and the night was blue black, with a million stars showing. Hugo had set his course by them, a skill he had learned in his youth in the desert. He was confident that their landfall was not far from the palace.

The coastline at this point was a series of small creeks divided by ridges of outcrop. Each of these indentations deepened, as it ran inland, into a gully full of bushes and small twisted trees. It was clear to Hugo that all he had to do was to follow one of these gullies for a few hundred yards, when he must strike the coast road, either between Mohara and the palace or between the palace and the Metbor workings. He would know for certain when he hit the road: from Mohara to the palace it was a paved two-lane highway; north of the palace it degenerated into a track.

He explained all this to Tammy in a whisper as they lugged the boat up onto the sand. She said, "What about me?"

"You'll be much safer here."

"I feel safer when I'm with you."

"Someone's got to look after the boat. It's got our stuff in it."

"I'm not worried about our stuff. I'm worried about me."

Hugo considered reminding her that she had promised to do what he said. The thought of conducting a long argument in whispers decided him against it. He said weakly, "All right. But keep very quiet."

The first twenty yards was easy. Then the trouble began. The ground underfoot started to get soft. At one point Hugo sank in up to his thighs and thought, in a moment of panic, that he had struck a patch of quicksand. Behind him, Tammy said, "Remember I'm shorter than you. If this gets much worse, I'll disappear altogether."

"We'll try the side."

The bank was firmer, but covered with a mat of prickly

165

bushes. Both of them had bare legs, and Hugo heard Tammy gasp once or twice. He said, "Wait here for a moment. I'm going to see what it's like at the top."

He forced his way straight up the side. The last few yards were nearly vertical, and he had to go on hands and knees, but the bushes were thinner. On top there was a sort of track. As he stood there, he sensed a lightening of the darkness ahead of him. The moon was coming up.

He heard an anxious whisper in the darkness below him, and said, "It's all right. I'm still here. And I think I've found a path."

"Well, thank the Lord."

He stretched out a hand and pulled her up. She said, "Just give a girl two minutes for urgent repairs. I'd like to get some of these thorns out."

"Not too long," said Hugo. "It's getting lighter every moment."

The path twisted and turned and was completely overgrown in places, but it was a path. Ten minutes of it brought them out into the open. The rising moon shed its cold light onto a stretch of paved road. They were south of the palace.

"Thank God for civilization," said Tammy.

Hugo looked at her. She was black to the knees with caked mud and her legs were scratched and bleeding. Her thin dress was ripped in several places.

"You don't look much better yourself," she said.

"We're a pair," agreed Hugo. They set off down the road.

"What do we do when we get to the palace?"

"If the ruler's in control, they'll let us in. If the other side are there, we turn back and make for the town."

The truck that came round the corner toward them was running without lights. They heard it in time to get into the ditch beside the road. It rocketed past them and disappeared in the direction of Mohara.

"Who was it?" said Tammy. "Them or us?"

"I was too busy getting into the ditch to notice," said Hugo. "I'm pretty certain it wasn't a police truck."

"I didn't think so either," said Tammy. They walked on in silence for some time, each busy with private thoughts.

166

There was a cluster of huts round the outside of the palace walls, primitive affairs, walled and roofed with woven palm fiber. They were close to these when the second truck arrived. It came out of the battlemented entrance of the palace, and they heard the heavy inner door clang shut behind it. This time there was no convenient ditch, so they stepped into the shadow of one of the huts. This truck, too, was traveling without lights but it was moving more slowly. As it passed them, they saw that it was packed with men standing at the back. They were carrying rifles, but no one could have mistaken them for soldiers or policemen. They were shouting and laughing, and as they went past, one or two of them loosed off shots. They seemed to be aiming at a line of posts in the space between the huts and the palace wall.

Hugo and Tammy stood, unmoving and silent, while the truck accelerated and drove off down the road, and the noise of its progress diminished and died away in the distance.

"That looked pretty conclusive to me," said Tammy at last.

"Yes," said Hugo.

"The rebs have got hold of the palace. I guess that little crowd was off to whoop it up in the town. But they won't have left the palace unguarded." She added, "What do you think?" because Hugo didn't seem to be listening to her. And then, "Where are you going now?"

"I want to look at those posts they were shooting at," said Hugo. "You'd better stay where you are. There may be people watching from the walls."

He moved along behind the row of huts, keeping in the shadow. When he reached the last one, he was still ten yards from the nearest post, but the moonlight was bright enough for him to see. The sacklike object up against each of the posts was a man, lashed to it by cords round the body and legs, with arms twisted behind it. The men were all in the uniform of the palace guard, and the way they were hanging made it clear they were dead.

He moved slowly back the way he had come. Tammy said, "They were our men, weren't they? They'd been executed."

"Yes," said Hugo. "We'd better get under cover while we think out what to do next."

He tried the door of the nearest hut. It swung open. They went in cautiously. There was no movement inside, and the hut seemed to be empty. It took them a few moments to adjust to the gloom of the interior. Then, by the moonlight filtering through the cracks in the walls, they began to take in some of the details. A cooking stove in the far corner, a cupboard, with a door hanging open as if it had been forced, a table still covered with the remains of a meal, one chair upright and one over-turned. A door at the back gave onto a lean-to which might have been sleeping quarters.

Hugo said, "I don't think there's anyone here, but I'd better make sure."

The back room was darker than the front. Hugo got out his cigarette lighter and clicked it on, holding it in front of him. There were two people in the room. A man was lying on the floor in the corner. His head had been smashed in. A young girl was lying on the bed. She was lying half on her face. Her hands had been tied behind her. Hugo heard Tammy come in and clicked off the lighter. He said, "Let's get out of here."

When they were back in the front room, Tammy said, "They're both dead, aren't they?"

"Yes," said Hugo.

"What are you planning to do about it?"

"What I want to do," said Hugo," is get into that palace and kill someone."

"And just how are you going to do that? Knock down the front door with your thick head? Or fly over the walls, like Batman?" Hugo looked at her in surprise. She was shaking with fury, or shock; or a mixture of both. "And when you get there, what are you planning to do, you gorgeous great brute. Savage them with your claws, or tear out their throats with your teeth?"

"For God's sake," said Hugo, "keep your voice down."

"Let's have a plan. Let's have a wonderful, all-star, Tech-nicolor plan for getting us out of this goddamned mess you've got us into."

168

The light was brighter than the moon. It was penetrating every crack in the flimsy wall. A voice outside shouted something. It sounded like English. They caught the words, "Come on out." Then there was a burst of automatic fire. The bullets tore a hole out of the wall as they threw themselves flat on the floor.

"Next time, lower down," said the voice. Hugo crawled to the door and pushed it open. Twenty yards away, a parked truck was pointing toward them, with its headlights on. He climbed slowly to his feet.

"Come on, come on," said the voice impatiently.

Hugo walked forward. Behind the lights was a little group of men. He had already recognized the voice. It was Dr. Kassim, but a very different figure from the dapper civilian he had last seen in Moharram's store. The doctor was in Arab soldier's uniform. A pistol hung from either side of his belt and he had a machine gun slung across his chest.

He said something in Arabic and two men ran into the hut with their rifles at the ready. They came out, shaking their heads and laughing.

Dr. Kassim jerked his head toward the palace. Two men grabbed Hugo by an arm each. Several of them took hold of Tammy. There seemed to be competition for that job. Dr. Kassim followed. Hugo noticed that he was limping badly. Hugo and Tammy were hustled through the gateway, into the courtyard, and backed up against the wall. Half a dozen guns were pointing at them.

Dr. Kassim said, "I warned you once. Now you will be shot. I think we will shoot the girl first, so you can watch, eh?"

Hugo said nothing.

"My men are not good shots. Perhaps they will shoot her first in the stomach. Then she will roll around a bit. Maybe they will find it difficult to hit her. That will be amusing for you to watch. It might take half an hour before they finish her off."

It was the moment, thought Hugo. The moment for a gesture. A scornful retort. Do what you like, you swine. You won't make either of us crawl to you. But his mouth was dry. He had no words to say. He knew that if he could save their lives by crawling, he would crawl the length of the compound. Dr. Kassim was watching him closely, a very slight smile on his lips.

One of the men said something to Dr. Kassim. He turned his head to listen. When he turned it back, he was looking at Tammy.

He said, "This girl is American? A friend of Mr. Ringbolt?"

"Yes."

"It is possible she might be more useful to us alive." Then he said, in Arabic, "Take them below. We will see in the morning."

As Hugo grasped the meaning of the words, his heart seemed to turn right over. The morning? The morning was seven or eight hours away. He had been presented with seven or eight hours of life. It was the finest present he had ever been given.

They were grabbed and hustled through an opening in the side of the archway. A flight of stone steps led into a passage that had a number of doors with small gratings in them. Hugo imagined that they must have been cellars for the storage of food and fuel. He and Tammy were pushed into one of these. There was a semicircular opening in the far wall, at head height. It was heavily barred, but the full moon, shining directly through it, gave enough light for them to see that except for a stack of firewood in one corner, the room was empty.

One of the men who was holding Tammy pointed to the stack of wood and laughed. The other said what sounded like the Arabic word for "bed." This seemed to put an idea into his head.

Still holding one of Tammy's arms twisted behind her back, he put up his free hand, caught her dress at the neckband, and ripped it open.

Hugo shook off the men who were holding him and jumped forward. He gave one of Tammy's captors a swinging blow in the stomach and grabbed hold of the other by the hair. The next moment, they were all three rolling on the floor.

It was only the fact that it was dark and that there were too many of them and that they got in each other's way that saved Hugo from getting badly hurt in the next few minutes. A random kick landed on the side of his head. He was dimly conscious that something was happening. There was a burst of rifle fire

170

above. Orders were being screamed out. The door of their cell banged shut and he heard the lock click. Running footsteps, then silence.

Tammy was crouched beside him, wiping the blood from his face with a piece of her torn dress.

Hugo rolled over, got his knees under him, and levered himself slowly to his feet. The bright yellow moon, which had been circling round him, steadied in its orbit.

Tammy said, "Can you walk?"

"I think so," said Hugo.

His legs took him across to the woodpile and he sat down on it. Tammy sat beside him. Outside, the firing had stopped and everything was quiet.

Chapter 20 / The Power of Money

It was Tammy who spoke first. She said, "I'm sorry."

Hugo stared at her. The mist was clearing gradually. He could see straight, and was beginning to hear things.

He ran the tip of his tongue round his lips and licked off the blood. Most of it came from a tooth which had been knocked out. He put up a hand to feel the back of his head. There was a lump there, the size of a tennis ball, and more blood matting his hair. That seemed to be the main damage.

He said, "It's not you who should be sorry. It's me. I've been a bloody imbecile. A cretin. A one-man goon show."

"All the same, I shouldn't have lost my temper. You were doing what you thought was right."

"Oh, I meant well," said Hugo. "What an epitaph." His anger was effectively clearing his head. "I suppose you realize that there's just one thing we've got to do. We've got to get out of this bloody place. And bloody quick. I don't know what's happening up top, and I don't know who's in charge, but sooner or later they're going to start thinking about what to do with us. And before that happens, I'd like to be gone."

"Me, too," said Tammy.

She had knotted up the front of her dress, and sat perched on the edge of the woodpile, looking like a good little girl waiting to be told what to do next. She said, "I suppose, if we moved all these logs, we shouldn't find a trap door underneath leading to a forgotten tunnel."

"Only in television," said Hugo, and began to laugh.

Tammy looked at him anxiously.

"It's all right," he said. "I was just remembering the last episode I did. The situation was very similar. But of course the Tiger and his girl friend got out. It was dead simple."

"How?"

Hugo explained how. Tammy said, "If you think I'm going to take off all my clothes and lie on the floor waiting for those men to come back, you can think again."

"It wouldn't be very practical," agreed Hugo. He got up and went across to the door. "And we're not going to burrow our way out like the Count of Monte Cristo, either. It's the door or the window. I say, come and look at this."

"What?"

"The lock's on the inside."

"Is that something we ought to get excited about?"

They peered down at the lock. It was a solid iron box, fastened to the equally solid wooden door by a screw at each of the four corners.

Hugo was looking at it thoughtfully. Then he said, "That's it. Of course. It's on the inside because this is a cellar, not a prison cell. It's designed to keep people out, not to keep them in."

"Right now, it's doing both pretty well."

"On the contrary. All we'd need would be a fairly large screwdriver. Remove those four screws and the whole lock comes off. Then we open the door and walk out."

"Unless it's bolted on the outside, too."

"Did you hear them bolting it when they went out?"

"No. I don't think so. All I heard was the noise of the door being locked. It made quite a lot of noise."

"It's a heavy lock," said Hugo.

"And I don't suppose you carry a large screwdriver around with you?"

Hugo was feeling in his pockets. From one he took out a packet with three cigarettes in it, and his cigarette lighter. From the other a handkerchief, a small silver pencil, and a pair of dark glasses. Tammy contributed a purse from the side pocket of her dress. From it she produced a stub of lipstick, a very small nail file, and three or four coins.

173

"As an escape kit," said Hugo, "it's inadequate. That nail file might be useful."

"It's pretty fragile. I don't think you'd turn those screws with it."

Hugo inserted the thick end of the nail file into the slot in one of the screws and applied pressure. The only thing that twisted was the nail file.

After a minute of this, he abandoned the door and moved across to the window.

This was a semicircular opening, high up in the outer wall. The top was arched and the base was a slope of brickwork running up at a sharp angle. It was guarded by two grilles of iron bars.

The inner grille was formed of uprights only, embedded in the brickwork at top and bottom. The outer one was more elaborate. It was formed of two horizontal strips of metal which held the uprights rigid, and these were, in turn, sunk into the side walls at both their ends.

Hugo said, "It's helpful, up to a point, because the really tough grille is the outside one. If we could shift two of these inner bars it would give us space enough to squeeze through. At least, I think it would."

"What's the point of squeezing through one set of bars if there's another much worse set beyond?"

"The point is that once we've got one of these bars out, we've got a tool we could use to loosen the others."

He felt along the bricks which formed the inner edge of the slope, scratching with his fingernail at the mortar between them. Most of it was iron hard, but he thought he could detect a slight crumbling between the bricks at the left-hand end. He said, "We'll try your nail file on this one."

It was a painfully slow job, made no easier by difficulty in concentrating. Subconsciously he was listening, all the time, for the clatter of footsteps down the passage, the rattle at the door, the irruption of more violence and hatred and death.

The walls of the old palace were so thick that they could hear very little of what was going on above. Occasionally they heard

174

a voice shouting, and once a scream, high-pitched and thin, like the cry of a sea bird, cut off abruptly.

"How's it going?" said Tammy. "Can I do a bit?"

"What you could be doing," said Hugo, "is searching through that pile of logs to see if you can find a piece with some sort of point to it. Even a large splinter would be better than nothing. This file of yours is splendid for scratching and picking, but if I tried to use it as a lever I'd snap it for sure."

"Some of these logs are pretty jagged. I might be able to tear off a few bits."

"What with?"

"My teeth," said Tammy. "I've got good teeth."

It took him half an hour to shift the first brick. By the time it came away, the tips of his fingers were torn and his wrist was aching, but he felt a sense of achievement. It was cooled by a sight of what lay behind.

The bar he was attacking was the one at the extreme left-hand side of the opening and therefore the shortest. Its bottom end was embedded behind the second row of bricks and, as Hugo saw when he examined it closely with the help of his cigarette lighter, by a malevolent freak of the builder it had been placed behind the join in two bricks. Moreover, unlike the outer row, these had been laid end on and offered a much reduced point of attack.

"What's wrong?" said Tammy.

Hugo tried to explain, but found that he had some difficulty in forming the words.

"A header," he said. "That's what bricklayers call it. Because it's head on."

His tongue seemed suddenly to be thick, almost filling his mouth.

"Yes, I can see that," said Tammy.

"More difficult to shift."

"We got the first one out. We'll shift the next two, never fear. You can take time out. I'm going to spell you."

Hugo surrendered the nail file and sat down on the floor with his back to the log pile. His neck had started to ache and there was a dull pain in the back of his head. To ease it, he cupped his chin in one hand. His head felt so heavy that it was an effort to hold it up.

A shaking on his shoulder brought him round. He had slipped over sideways and was lying on the floor. He got onto his knees and then back onto his feet and said, "For God's sake. How long have I been out? What time is it?"

"You've been asleep for an hour," said Tammy. "I thought it was time to wake you up. I've got another brick out."

She held it out for inspection, but it wasn't the brick he was staring at. He said, "What have you done to your hands?"

"They're all right," said Tammy. "Look at my nice brick."

"They're not all right. You've torn them to ribbons. Why the hell didn't you wake me up? Give me that file at once."

When he tried to take it, he found it was stuck to the palm of her hand with blood. He said, "You let me snore on the floor for an hour while you did that."

"It seems to have done you some good. When you sat down you sounded like your battery was going flat or something."

"I'm all right," said Hugo. In fact, he felt a lot better. And the next brick was much easier. Since it was completely free on one side, Hugo was able to concentrate on the firm edge. He developed a technique for whittling a small hole in the mortar and driving in a splinter of wood, using the heel of his shoe as a hammer. After twenty minutes, he felt the brick shift.

"It's coming," he said.

Tammy was standing behind him as he eased it out. When he clicked on his lighter, they stood for a moment staring. Tammy said, "Oh," and then, "That's not so good." It was a reflex gasp of disappointment.

What they could now see was that the bottom end of the bar had been beaten out into a flat, spadelike section. A hole had been bored through the center and a bolt inserted. They could see the head of the bolt. The shank ran into the brickword.

"For God's sake," said Tammy. "What are we going to do about that?" There were tears not very far away.

"What we're not going to do," said Hugo, "is lose heart. I

don't believe that bolt can be very firm. It's only driven into the mortar. It was obviously put there to stop sideways movement of the bottom of the bars. I think it wouldn't be too difficult to pull it out."

As he said this, he was taking off his belt. It was a good leather belt with a steel buckle. He fastened one end round the bar, using the buckle, took the other end in both hands, braced his feet against the wall, exerted his fine dorsal muscles, and pulled.

"It's coming," he said. "I can feel it shifting. Lend a hand and we'll have the bastard out."

Tammy grabbed him round the waist from behind and heaved. Hugo heaved. The bar came loose at both ends with a sudden jerk.

"I hope I didn't hurt you," said Hugo.

"Not at all," said Tammy politely. "If you wouldn't mind getting off my stomach."

They picked up their trophy. It was about thirty inches long and was, as they saw when they examined the top end, hollow. A tube rather than a bar.

Tammy said, "Lovely. And the flattened end will just do for getting under those bricks." And when Hugo said nothing, "Only we ought to get a move on. We've got to shift three more bricks before we can even start on that outer grille. And that looks pretty tough to me."

Hugo still said nothing. He was staring at the iron tube. He looked at the long bolt running through the flattened end. Then he turned it round and examined the hollow at the top.

He said, "I don't think we're going to get those other bricks out in time. But I believe I might be able to open the door."

"Break it down, you mean?"

"No. Open it." He was prodding at the end of the tube with the nail file. "Do you see? It's hollow all the way down. What would you say the diameter of the hole was?"

"Do you mean, how wide is it?"

"That's what I mean."

"About an inch. Maybe a little less."

"That would be my guess."

"So what do we do?"

"We fill it with brick dust."

Tammy stared at him.

"Come on, come on," said Hugo. "Brick dust or mortar. There's plenty of it on the floor. Scoop it up. I'll be making a funnel. We'll use this cigarette packet. It should do."

Tammy said, "I suppose you know what you're doing."

"It all depends— That's right. If I hold the funnel, you dribble the stuff in. It won't take very much. Kind of them to flatten the other end. Saves us having to cork it up."

"You were saying," said Tammy, "that it all depended. *What* does it depend on? I mean, I trust you implicitly. But I'd just like to know. Girlish curiosity, I guess."

"It depends," said Hugo, "on what sort of money you've got in that purse of yours."

"Money?"

"That's right. I remember my partner, Colonel Rex, once saying to me, 'If you've got the right sort of money, you can buy your way out of anything.' "

"Hugo," said Tammy. "If you're just putting on this act to cheer me up, don't do it. I'm not in a fit state to be cheered up. If I get really mad, I might use this bar on you. I'd regret it afterwards, I don't doubt."

"Let's see the color of your money."

Tammy sighed. "All right," she said. "Don't say I didn't warn you." She tipped the contents of her purse into Hugo's cupped hands. "It's mostly small change I had left over from when I was in England."

"English money is the best in the world. The strongest and the most reliable. Let's see. A penny, a twopenny, and a five-penny bit. An excellent selection. The twopenny looks the best bet." He fitted the coin, endways on, into the mouth of the hollow bar. "A fraction too big, which is just what the doctor ordered. Hold the bar upright while I get my shoe off again."

Using the heel of his shoe as a hammer, he banged the coin down into the tube until its lower rim was resting firmly on the packed brick dust and only its upper semicircle was projecting from the tube.

178

"I'm beginning," said Tammy, "to get the idea. Ow! That was my finger, if you don't mind. Won't it tip over when you start to use it?"

"It might, if we let it. But we won't. Here's where we want those wood splinters. The very small ones first." He drove in half a dozen of them, using the silver pencil as a rammer and tamping them down with his shoe. "Now a larger one for the other side. That one will do the trick, I think. There she is. The Greest homemade screwdriver, Mark One."

Tammy, who was sucking the tips of her fingers, said, "I hope we don't need a Mark Two. Do you think it'll work?"

"It's got to," said Hugo soberly. He was wrapping his handkerchief round the crossbolt which ran through the flattened end of the bar. "We can get a lot of leverage with this. Hold the lighter so that I can see the enemy."

Hugo fitted the edge of the coin into the slot of one of the big screws which held the lock mechanism of the door in place. He was annoyed to find that he was trembling so much that he needed both hands to keep it steady. Then he gripped the crossbolt and exerted pressure. For an agonizing moment, nothing happened. Then he said, "It's shifting. We've got the bugger."

"Glory be," said Tammy.

The two screws on the right side of the lock came out without too much difficulty. The third, which was the bottom one on the left, stuck fast. Either it had been driven into a knot of the wood, or it had rusted in with particular firmness.

Hugo refixed the handkerchief, gripped the crossbolt even more firmly, and twisted. The sweat was pouring down his neck and arms. He felt a slight movement, and hope flickered. Then he realized that it was the coin, not the screw, that was shifting.

"So near," he said, "and yet so far." He was panting so that he could hardly get the words out. The big muscles in his arms had started to go back on him and his hands were shaking badly.

"Hold on a minute," said Tammy. She was watching him anxiously. "I have an idea. It's that third bastard screw that's stopping us. Right?"

"Right," said Hugo. He was getting his breath back. The sweat on his neck and arms was cooling.

"Then what do you say you leave it alone and try the fourth one?"

"I could. But why?"

"If it comes out, there'll just be one last screw holding the whole thing. Right? The lock will be pivoting on that screw. So you give it a smack with the bar and it'll start to twist. That'll soon bring it loose, you see."

"Tammy," said Hugo, "you're a genius. And I'm an idiot."

The fourth screw came away without difficulty. Hugo clouted the lock twice and it started to move. A few more cracks and the final obstinate screw gave up the unequal struggle. The whole of the lock mechanism came away in Hugo's hands and the door swung open.

They peered out into the passage. It was empty and dark. Until this moment it had not occurred to either of them to consider what they were going to do next.

Chapter 21 / A Night and a Day—

"Where now?" said Tammy, speaking very softly.

"No good going back up the stairs," said Hugo. "That comes out in the main gateway. It's bound to be guarded. We'll try the other way and see what happens."

"I guess it'll just lead to more cellars."

"We can find somewhere to hide up."

"I suppose so," said Tammy.

"Come on then."

"Hold it a moment."

They stood in silence. Then Hugo heard what Tammy's sharper ears had picked up already. It came from the next cellar. It was something between a gasp and a groan, a muted sound, disturbing by implication; a cry muttered, a scream suppressed.

"Poor devil," said Hugo. "I wonder who it is."

"Ought we to find out?"

"Maybe we ought. If you'll tell me how we're going to break down the door."

"I suppose that's right," said Tammy. She went over to the grating in the door to listen. Then she turned the handle gently and pushed. The door swung open.

The moon lit up the inside of the cellar and they saw Prince Hussein. He was fastened, by a shackle round his left wrist, to a chain which ran up to a staple in the wall. The chain was so short that it held his arm above his head.

"We'll soon have the boy out of that," said Hugo. It was only when he came close that he saw there was something wrong with the arm.

Hussein said, "It's broken."

They stared in blank disbelief.

"You mean to say," said Tammy, "they've hitched him up by his broken arm? For God's sake."

Hugo looked at the boy. His face was drained of color. He guessed that Hussein must be very near to passing out. The thought of what would happen if he did faint, and put all his weight on the broken bone, turned Hugo's stomach.

He said, "We can get him out, but it'll have to be done very carefully. We've got to avoid any pressure on that arm. What I'm going to do is lift the boy up in my arms until the chain is quite slack. You then push the thin end of the bar through the staple in the wall, put all your weight on the flat end—wrap this handkerchief round the crossbolt; it'll give you a firm grip—and put your weight on the bar."

It was a good idea. What was wrong with it was Tammy's weight.

After a long minute, she said, "It moved a little. I'll swear it did. I doubt if I'll ever get it out, though."

"All right. We change places. You'll have to hold Hussein. Not in your arms. I don't think you're strong enough. I'm going to put him pickaback on your shoulders."

"I'm all right," said Hussein faintly. "A little jerk on my arm won't kill me."

"It won't be necessary. Kneel down, Tammy. That's right. I'm going to put his legs over your shoulders. Get hold of his ankles. Then I'm going to lift him while you straighten up. Right?"

"Right," said Tammy. It came out like a gasp.

When they were in position, Hugo picked up the bar and pushed it right through the staple until the flat end was resting on the wall. Then he got one foot against the wall, gripped the other end of the bar in both hands, and heaved with all the considerable strength of his shoulder muscles. The staple came out like a cork out of a bottle.

Hugo picked himself up off the floor. He said, "The next thing

182

is to make some sort of sling. We'll have to use a piece of Hussein's robe. Have you got that nail file?" He worked the point into the cloth, tore out a long strip, knotted it round Hussein's neck, and eased his left arm into the fold. "We can't do much about the chain. Tuck it inside your shirt. Let's get moving."

As they were walking across to the door, Hussein said, "Thank you, Mr. Greest."

"You can thank me when we're out of here," said Hugo. "We've a long way to go."

"We will get out now. It will not be too difficult. I will show you."

"What do you mean?"

"I will show you the way."

At the cellar door he turned left, away from the stairs they had come down. As soon as they left the area of the door, they were in blackest darkness.

"It will be better if we keep hold of each other," said Hussein. Hugo held the back of his shirt. Tammy grabbed Hugo's arm. They went forward very slowly. They turned a corner. A long time afterward, they turned a second corner. They seemed to be going downhill.

Hugo felt his feet slipping and saved himself by grabbing Tammy's arm with his free hand.

Hussein said, "It is damp. You must walk carefully." And a little later, "The smell will not be good. I am sorry."

"No need to apologize," said Hugo.

There was an inch of slime underfoot now. The smell was far from good.

Hussein had stopped. He seemed to be feeling the wall with the fingers of his right hand. He said, "When I was a young boy, I knew all these cellars and passages. My father did not like me getting out of the palace. There were five or six ways I could get out. He had them all blocked up. But this one he never found."

"I don't really blame him," said Hugo. "Would it be safe to use a light?"

"You have an electric torch?"

"I've got a cigarette lighter."

"That, no. A flame might ignite the gas. No matter, I have found what I want. We go ten paces forward from here. We may sink down a little. It will be better not to breathe too much."

Ahead of them was a faint grayness. It was hardly a light, more a shading of the dead blackness in which they moved. As they went forward, Hugo felt himself sinking, first to his calves, then to his knees in the indescribable filth which had accumulated at the bottom of this sump.

Hussein stopped. He was staring upward at what was clearly an air vent. The opening was level with their heads, and it sloped upward and outward at a sharp angle. The top, they could see now, was blocked by a grid.

Hussein said, "I drove in small pieces of iron. You can feel them with your hands. It is quite easy to climb. When you reach the top, you will find the grating unfastened."

Quite easy to climb, thought Hugo. For someone with two good arms that might be true. But what about Hussein? He put that problem on one side for the moment.

Once he had started, it was not difficult. He simply felt for the next handhold and foothold and hoisted his way up. When he reached the grating, he got his shoulders under and heaved. It was held down only by the weeds and small bushes which were choking the outlet, and pivoted open.

Hugo extracted himself cautiously. He had surfaced behind the palace, and some fifty yards from it. The moon was more than half way through its nightly orbit, fading in glory now, but still strong enough to pale the stars.

Hugo took three deep, slow breaths, and then turned to the problem in hand.

It was clear that Hussein would have to be lifted out, and that his left arm would have to be disturbed as little as possible during the operation. Reduced to these essentials, the only possible answer presented itself. Hugo went back down the way he had come. He said to Tammy, "First we will get Hussein onto my shoulders. Then you go ahead up the slope and stop, lying on your face. Your feet should just about be level with this end

184

of the pipe. We're going to use your body as a sledge, if you follow me. I shall provide the motive power from behind. If I keep Hussein tilted over on his right side, he can use his good arm to latch onto you. You'd better put it round her neck, Hussein."

"I cannot put you to such trouble, Mr. Greest. Better for me to stay here while you fetch help."

"Either we all stay or we all go," said Hugo. "And if we stay here, we shall be asphyxiated in five minutes. So stop arguing. I'll crouch down and you hoist him up, Tammy. But for God's sake be quick, my mouth's almost in this muck."

They got Hussein up somehow. Tammy climbed into the pipe, and the ascent began. It was agonizingly slow, but not impossibly difficult. Hugo heard Hussein gasp once as his broken arm scraped the roof. Then they were all out, and lying on the sand.

"Not much more than an hour of darkness," said Hugo. "We've got to move." He wondered if Tammy felt as tired as he did. Hussein must have been in great pain, but he was giving no sign of it.

"I'm going to put this grating back and clear up the mess a bit. Then we'll circle round until we hit the road. We've got to find our boat before it gets light."

It took them half an hour to find the road, moving very cautiously and keeping out of sight of the palace battlements. When they reached the road, there was no sign of movement, but they decided against using it.

"If a truck did come along," said Hugo, "we'd never get into the ditch in time. Hussein's in no shape for gymnastics. We'll have to move off the road, parallel to it, and keep our eyes open for that track."

Keeping their eyes open was becoming disturbingly easier. The dawn was coming up fast.

"If we don't strike it soon," said Tammy, "I guess we'd better get into the bush any old way. I'm beginning to feel a mite exposed."

"Push on a bit," said Hugo. "I think we're coming to it."

185

There were a number of gullies leading down toward the shore, all choked with bushes and scrub, all looking very like one another. "The path we came up by," said Hugo, "ran along the top of quite a steep ridge. A sort of hogback, and there was a clump of palm trees where it came out onto the road. I think this is it."

"If you say so," said Tammy doubtfully.

They made their way along the path for some distance. Hugo had one arm round Hussein, holding him up. Tammy went ahead, forcing a way through the lacing undergrowth. They all felt happier to be clear of the main road.

The path kept to the crest of the ridge but dipped steadily. They had made about a quarter of a mile and Hugo was beginning to wonder if he had been right, when Tammy stopped. It was quite light now.

She said, "Bang on, boy scout. This is where we climbed up. I'm sure of it. You can see the scrapes we left."

"Fine," said Hugo. "I'll go down first. Hussein can slide over on his stomach and I'll help him down from below. It's only the first piece that's steep."

When he got down, he found even clearer proof that they were in the right spot. He could see the marks left in the sand by his own shoes.

"Not far now," he said.

It was easier, in the daylight, to avoid the rocks and the treacherous patches of mud. In five minutes, they broke through the last line of bushes and came out onto the seashore. It took them a few heart-stopping seconds to realize that their boat was gone.

"Well," said Tammy, "what do we do now?"

Hussein said nothing. He simply looked toward Hugo. His confidence was unshaken.

What did they do next? Hugo consulted his dazed and tired brain. The three things he wanted were a bath, a long drink, and twelve hours' sleep. Two of these might be managed, after a fashion. He said, "I think the first thing is to clean up a bit. Then we'll find somewhere to get under cover."

186

"We're none of us pretty," agreed Tammy. In the cold light of morning this was seen to be less than the truth. Her dress had been a light summer number, suitable for a picnic. What was left of the top was tied in a rough knot over her breast. The bottom was torn to shreds. Her legs showed a solid surface of mud and filth, broken by trickles of blood. Hugo was in better shape only because his jacket and shoes had stood up better to the night's work. Hussein looked like the survivor of a lost battle, his clothes in rags, his arm in a sling, his face the color of paper, his feet bare and bleeding.

The first part of the program was the easiest. Hugo and Tammy made Hussein sit down, and washed his feet and legs for him. Then they took off their own clothes, walked out into the sea, and washed themselves down. They then came back, used their discarded clothes as towels, and put them on again.

Finding somewhere to lie low was not so easy. The bushes were not tall enough to give much shade. They were cool at the moment, with their bathe and their damp clothes, but before long the need for shade was going to be paramount.

"We'll have to build something," said Hugo. He found a flat space on the north side of a ridge of outcrop, cleared away the loose stones, and pulled up the small bushes until they had room to lie down. Then he and Tammy pulled up other bushes to make some sort of head cover. It was unpleasant work for torn hands.

At last they lay down to try to get some sleep. Fatigue fought against the flies, and the flies soon won.

Hugo was uncertain whether he slept at all. At best it was a short, uneasy doze. He rolled over, groaned, and sat up. The others were both awake.

Tammy said, "Speaking personally, I could do with a drink."

Hugo realized, then, how thirsty he was himself. He said, "There must be houses. In fact, I think I saw one, a bit back from the road, just beyond where we turned off. A house means water. I'll scout around. You keep an eye on Hussein."

"No need if you don't wish," said Hussein. "I shall be all right by myself."

187

"You don't look all right to me," said Tammy. "You look like something the cat's dragged in and left on the hearth rug."

"You don't look so hot yourself," said Hussein with something of his old spirit.

"If you're going to argue," said Hugo, "keep your voices down." He got stiffly to his feet and started off.

At the top of the track, he stopped and examined the road cautiously. It was suspiciously quiet. The last time he had driven along it, there had been a continuous stream of cars, carts, and bicyclists. Now it was deserted. He could hear, in the distance, from the direction of Mohara, the rattle of machine gun fire and what sounded like the *crump* of mortar shells. This made him think. He was fairly certain that Martin Cowcroft had told him that neither side possessed mortars. It looked as though one side had got hold of them. This meant that some, at least, of the consignment of arms had been landed.

If the rebels were centered on the palace area and the royalists were holding the town, he was behind the enemy lines, and it was clearly his job to get back to Mohara as quickly as possible. It could be managed during the hours of darkness that night. The fighting lines would not be continuous, and the rough belt of scrub along the shore extended almost to the outskirts of the town. Alone, he could do it. But not with a girl and a cripple.

The road in front of him remained quiet and empty. Hugo got up and made his way along it, keeping to the verge on the left side, ready to dive into cover the moment danger threatened.

The house he was making for was a white-walled, red-tiled building standing back from the road and partly masked by palm trees. It was not, as he had first thought, a farmhouse. It was a fairly pretentious villa, and was surrounded by a head-high wall with a spiked railing on the top. The ironwork gates were locked. It was not a formidable obstacle. Hugo got his hand through the bars and lifted the bolt which went into the ground and held one gate. Then he kicked the other until it opened.

All the ground-floor windows in front were barred. Above them a balcony ran round three sides of the house. It looked like

188

an open invitation to an active burglar. You used the crossbars of the window as a foothold, hoisted yourself onto the balcony, and broke in by a second-story window.

Before putting this to the test, he walked round to the back of the house to see if there was an easier way in. Here there was a courtyard, with sheds round two sides, and in one of the sheds he found the well. Peering from the top, he could see no glint of water. He remembered Cowcroft telling him that where these aquifer springs existed they were sometimes two or three hundred feet deep. A pipe ran down the side. The water supply was clearly operated by an electric pump. Equally clearly the electricity had been turned off.

It was at this moment that he heard the noise. He had been vaguely conscious for some time of a grumbling. Now it sharpened into something like a bark. In the far corner of the yard a dog was lying in a patch of shade. It was attached by a length of chain to a ring in the wall. And it was nearly dead of thirst.

Hugo's feelings about the absent owners of the villa changed from curiosity to dislike. To have scuttled off in a panic in the face of the rebels was understandable. To have left their dog chained up to die of thirst put them outside the pale. Fortified by anger, he hoisted himself up onto the second-floor balcony, opened a French window by putting the sole of his foot through it, and started, with some enthusiasm, to commit the first burglary of his life.

Although the water pump had been turned off, there must still be a supply in the cistern. If the owners had left in a hurry, they would not have had time to drain it. Sure enough, when he turned on one of the bath taps, a gout of rust-colored water came out. He let it run until it had cleared, and then tasted it cautiously. It was brackish but drinkable. He splashed it over his face and hair and swallowed a good deal of it. The next problem was containers.

Rejecting flower vases, chamber pots, saucepans, a soup tureen, and a metal ice bucket as being either too bulky or too likely to spill, he finally unearthed half a dozen dusty but empty bottles from the bottom of the kitchen cupboard. They held about a pint each. He rinsed them out, filled them, and corked them. Then he put them into a straw shopping basket and fashioned a sling out of a roller towel so that he could carry the basket over his shoulder, leaving both his hands free.

After that he turned his mind to food. There was a big refrigerator. He opened the door, and shut it again hastily. The electricity must have been off for some time. He tried the cupboards.

The first two held kitchen stuff and china. In the last one there were some oddments of food. An unopened packet of Brekkibrix ("The Busy Man's Breakfast Food"), a tin of tomatoes, and a large brown-paper bag full of dates. Hugo divided the dates into two smaller packages, which he put in the side pockets of his jacket, belted his jacket in the top of his trousers, and let the Brekkibrix and the tomatoes slide down into the loop so formed. He remembered to take a can opener, too.

Fortunately the back door turned out to be bolted but not locked. He let himself out into the yard, clanking loudly at each step.

The dog gave a token growl when he approached, but was too weak to get up. Hugo unpacked the Brekkibrix and one bottle of water. He soaked two or three of the brix in water and put them down in front of the dog, who looked at them disinterestedly. Then he poured the rest of one of the bottles into the dog's drinking bowl. The dog staggered to its feet, buried its nose in the trough, and started lapping. Hugo slid his hand round the animal's neck and gently unfastened the clip which attached its collar to the chain.

He said, "You're on your own now, boy. Keep out of sight, don't let yourself get picked up by some hairy Arab who wants to slice you up for cat's meat, and you've got a fifty-fifty chance of coming through. Just the same as us, really."

The dog was too busy drinking to take any notice. Hugo wadded the remaining five bottles of water with palm leaves to stop them from clanking. Then he started back.

190

When Tammy saw him coming, she gave a croak of pleasure. "I hope you found that water," she said. "Another half hour and I'd have been drinking the sea."

"I got water. And food, of a sort." Hugo patted his stomach.

"You look like the hunchback of Notre Dame behind and a pregnant mum in front!"

"Never mind my appearance," said Hugo. "Let's get started on breakfast."

While he was away, Tammy had improved the camouflage of their hideout by adding tufts of grass to the brushwood roof. Hussein was lying underneath it, on his back. His eyes were open and his face was flushed and sweating. He drank the water but would eat nothing. Hugo opened the tin of tomatoes and tried a mixture of Brekkibrix and tomato juice. The taste was curious but not unpleasant. For a second course they ate some dates.

Tammy said, "Hussein has been telling me what happened at the palace. I guess perhaps he'd better put you wise."

Hugo said, "Don't talk now if you don't want to." Although the morning was already hot, the boy was both shivering and sweating. It was clear that he had a fever.

"I will tell you," said Hussein. "It was in the morning. Yesterday morning. The gate was open for the morning majlis. Three or four men came in together. They had pistols under their robes. They shot the gate guard. Then the others, who had been hiding nearby, rushed in. When the first shots were fired, Major Youba, who had charge of my uncle, Sheik Hammuz, shot him."

"Killed him?"

"Of course. Those were his orders."

Hugo said, "Don't describe the next bit if you'd rather not. I can guess the sort of things that happened."

"There was much shooting. My father was one of the first to be killed. After he was killed, some of the palace guard surrendered. Major Youba would not surrender, although he had been wounded. In the end they overpowered him and dragged him out. It was Dr. Kassim who arranged how he should die."

"Ah," said Hugo.

"Don't tell it again, Hussein," said Tammy. "It's horrible."

"No, I will tell you. He had the major tied to the muzzle of the gun. The big gun in the courtyard. Then he loaded it and fired it himself."

"How perfectly horrible."

"He didn't get off scot-free," said Hussein. "It crushed his foot. He'd forgotten that the—I don't know the name—the thing that controls the recoil?"

"The recuperator?"

"Yes. It would not be working too well after all those years. The gun jumped back and ran over his foot. It broke."

"Splendid."

"I was glad, too, and I said so. That was when Dr. Kassim had my arm broken. Then he had the prisoners from the royal guard taken out and tied to posts and they shot at them. They tried to see how much they could shoot at them without killing them. It took a long time. They made me watch."

Tears were running down the boy's face. Tammy said, "Stop thinking about it, Hussein. What's done is done. It's all over now. Try to get some sleep."

She made him lie down and sat beside him, stroking his head with one hand and using the other to keep the flies off his face. Hugo watched her with mixed feelings. After a time Hussein did seem to fall into an uneasy sleep.

Tammy said, "You realize we've got to get that arm set properly. I tried to dress it, but I couldn't do anything really. The end of the bone is sticking through the skin. If it isn't seen to, his arm's going bad, that's for sure."

"I've been thinking about that," said Hugo. "The first thing is to find out what's happening, and we can only do that in Mohara. When I was out just now I heard mortar fire. That means that some of the arms I was buying for the ruler have arrived. One planeload, perhaps. If our people got them, it gives the police the edge. But it means more than that. It means they've got the rebels pinned down outside the town. If they were rushing round the streets, killing and looting, you wouldn't attack them with mortars."

192

"That sounds sort of logical," said Tammy. "What do you suggest we do? Wait here till they've got things under control?"

"We can't do that. Because of Hussein, and because we may be spotted. I shall have to get into Mohara tonight. It shouldn't be too difficult. There won't be any fixed lines. This isn't trench warfare."

"And when you get there?"

"If our side's on top, I'll get them to lay on a patrol to come out here and pick you up. They'll certainly want to do that. He's all the ruler they've got left now."

"He's a fine boy," said Tammy. "He'll make a good king if we can get him through. What happens if things aren't so you can organize a rescue party?"

"I've thought about that, too. What I'll have to do is steal a boat and come back here myself. The best place to make for will be Oman. It's not too far, and the Oman Scouts would look after us."

"It sounds all right," said Tammy doubtfully. "*If* you can find a boat. And *if* you can get it up here."

"We'll cross those bridges when we come to them," said Hugo. He suddenly felt unreasonably cheerful. "I'm going to have another swim. You can be getting lunch ready. Brekkibrix-date-and-tomato stew."

Hours later, as the sun was at last going down, throwing long shadows over the sea, tipping the waves with sparks of fire, something moved, way out, between the light and the dark.

At first Hugo thought it was a mirage. Then, as it came closer, he saw it was a boat, and heard the beat of its engine.

"Better get our heads down," said Hugo. "They seem to be searching the shoreline."

The boat crept closer. It was a big diesel-powered craft towing a smaller one. Someone was standing up in the bow, raking the shore with a pair of field glasses.

"Good God!" said Hugo. "It's Charlie!" He jumped to his feet and ran down to the water's edge. As the boat swung toward them they saw that it was, indeed, Charlie Wandyke.

"We picked up your boat on the way down last night," said Charlie. "In fact, we nearly ran it down. I knew it was yours; you'd left a lot of your stuff in it. And I was fairly certain you were holed up somewhere on shore, so when I'd dumped my folk on the other side, I bribed the crew with a bottle of Scotch to come back and look for you."

The crew of two grinned. Hugo said, "I don't know how to thank you."

"No thanks needed. Those Hammuz tribesmen are bad medicine on dry land, but they haven't got a navy yet. The boy doesn't look in very good nick. We ought to get him to a doctor."

"And fast," said Tammy.

They were heading out for the Ducks. Hussein was wrapped in blankets on the floor of the boat. He was muttering in a feverish doze and Tammy was squatting beside him. They had strapped his broken arm across his body, and she was holding him to prevent him from turning onto it as the boat rolled.

"We'll put the islands between us and the mainland, and run straight down to Oman. The Scouts have got a headquarters camp at Bulair, on the coast. There'll be a doctor there."

"Have you any idea what's going on?"

"Not a clue. There were one or two fires in Mohara when we went past last night, but they were out when we came back this morning. I guess it was looting and the police got it back under control."

"If that's right," said Hugo, "and I think it must be, it means

194

that we're holding the town and they're holding the palace. If you could land me somewhere on the coast, south of the town, I could probably get in without a lot of difficulty."

"You've been lucky once," said Charlie. "Why take chances?"

"You don't seem to realize," said Hugo, "that I've got a job to do. I've made a bloody mess of it so far, but that doesn't mean I've got to stop trying."

"Up to you. Speaking personally, I'd give them two or three days to cut each other's throats and get it out of their systems. But then I'm just a coward. Could you manage something to eat?"

"I ought to be hungry," said Hugo. "But somehow I'm not. I think it was all those dates. I could manage a drink of something."

"Hot coffee?"

"Oh, boy!" said Tammy. "Did I hear someone say coffee?"

It was close to midnight. They had put Hussein and Tammy ashore at Bulair and made their way back along the coast. After a number of anxious conferences with his crew, Charlie had dropped anchor some way out from the shore.

"We can't take her in much closer," he said. "They tell me the bottom shelves very gradually here. You could swim and paddle ashore quite easily. Or if you want to save yourself from a ducking, take your own boat. Put the sail up and the night breeze will take you in."

"For a nonsailor," said Hugo, "you seem to know a good deal about this sort of thing."

"I've moved around a good deal. It's the job. You pick things up. Talking of which, have you got a gun?"

"I had one, but I left it behind in the flat. It didn't seem appropriate to take it on a picnic."

"That's the thing about guns. You only need them when you think you aren't going to. I'd better lend you this one. Look after it, won't you. I've had it a long time."

It was a Luger. Hugo handled it lovingly before slipping it inside his shirt.

"Eight shots in the clip," said Charlie, "and one up the spout, but the safety catch is on. Remember to push it off before you try to kill anyone with it."

"There's nothing you can tell me about a Luger," said Hugo. "It's my favorite weapon. I can't tell you how many foreigners I've finished off with one."

Charlie helped him to hoist the small sail on his boat and pushed him off in the direction of the shore. Hugo caught a last glimpse of the redoubtable metallurgist, outlined against the night sky, upright in the stern of the dhow. Then the wind filled the sail, the boat heeled over, and he was carried briskly toward the shore.

As Hugo was plodding up the beach, the sense of familiarity became stronger. A solitary rock, jutting out of the sea on his right, the line of the hummocks which marked the inland limit of the beach. He realized that he had landed, by chance, at the exact spot on which he had spent a peaceful day sunbathing. Nine days ago. It seemed a lot longer than that.

It was a stroke of luck, because now that he knew where he was, he could set a fairly accurate course. He was planning to move directly inland until he could see the southernmost outskirts of Mohara, then to make his way round, keeping on the fringe of the town, until he struck the police fort. If the resistance was being organized, that would be the heart of it.

It was only when he started to walk that he realized how tired he was. Apart from a short doze that morning, he had had no sleep for nearly forty-eight hours. Nor had they been restful hours. Oddly, it was the least dramatic episodes which came back to him most vividly. Not the horrors of the palace, but Tammy brushing the flies off Hussein's face, and the dog sniffing doubtfully at the Brekkibrix, and Hussein saying, "The smell will not be good." At this point he fell into a hole in the sand and realized that he had been walking for some time in his sleep.

He pulled himself together and tried to get his bearings. The clouds, which had been hiding the moon and the stars, were shredding away and there was no problem about direction. The difficulty was distance. He had no idea how far he had come.

196

He looked at his watch. He had been walking, or stumbling, for half an hour, and in that loose sand could not have covered much more than a mile. In normal times he should, by now, have had guidance from the lights of Mohara, but he imagined that it had become a city of the dead, with windows tightly shuttered and lights burning low.

He plodded on. Fatigue, and the intermittent appearances of the moon from behind the clouds, were combining to make his eyes play tricks. At one moment he was in the middle of a wide, empty stretch of desert. At the next, a long row of buildings had sprung up, away to his right. As he turned his head, the buildings slid away, too.

He said, "Bloody mirage. I shall be seeing visions soon. The cloud-capped towers, the gorgeous palaces, the solemn temples, the great globe itself, yea, all which it inherit shall dissolve, and like this insubstantial pageant, faded—"

On the word "faded," he tripped over a wire, a bell started ringing in the distance, and a blaze of white light enveloped him.

The shock cleared his head. He realized that he was on the edge of the airfield, and that a truck was coming toward him, fast. There was no point in running. He was held by the lights, transfixed in that wide open space.

He recognized the police uniforms as the men tumbled out of the truck and ran toward him. The first to arrive was Cowcroft's driver. The sergeant grinned and said, "Good to see you, Mr. Greest. We've been watching you for ten minutes, wondering who you were."

"I'm Father Christmas," said Hugo. "I lost my reindeer; that's why I had to walk. I was just planning to thumb a lift from the Queen of the Fairies when you came along."

The sergeant looked at him blankly and then said, "Jump in." They bowled back, their wheels humming along the tarmac air-strip. All the lights had gone out again, as suddenly as they had come on.

In the airport control room he found Martin Cowcroft and with him, somewhat to his surprise, Sayyed Nawaf.

Cowcroft said, "You look as if you've had a rough passage. We were very glad to hear you'd brought Prince Hussein back with you. We're going to need that young man."

"How did you know?"

"We've got a line through to Bulair. That's why we weren't surprised to see you. In fact, there's a patrol out looking for you now."

"If you're in touch with Oman, I suppose the Scouts could help you."

"They could. And if things had got bad enough, I expect they would, orders or no orders. But we don't need them."

"Then the rebels are beaten?"

"They're not finished yet. But they're on the run. The real hero was Sayyed Nawaf."

Nawaf smiled politely and said, "It was nothing. I was carrying out my master's orders. My late master's, I should say."

"He went straight off to Bahrain," said Cowcroft, "pulled every string in creation, and got that first planeload of arms diverted straight through to here. It had hardly touched down before he had it on its way again. He came back with it. At the first sign of trouble we took control of the airport, and we got the arms unloaded and distributed in time to give those bastards a bloody nose. They never got any lodgment in the town. The few who did get in didn't leave again. They've been sulking round outside and we've been hammering them with our mortars. Today we're going out to mop them up. The only real center of resistance is the palace. We shall have to blast them out of that somehow. It may be a bit expensive, but once we've got the palace back, the war's over."

"I can show you a cheap way in," said Hugo. "If you're not fussy about smells."

"What do you mean?"

Hugo explained what he meant. Cowcroft said, "It sounds all right. Can you explain how we find the place? Can we get there without being spotted?"

"There's no need for me to explain it, because I'm coming with you. And since I managed to get out with a girl and a one-armed boy, I suppose a few able-bodied men ought to be able to get in again."

Cowcroft considered the matter. He said, "Just before sunup will be best. We don't want to start the fight until it's light. Night fighting's too messy, particularly with inexperienced troops. We'll go in at half-past five. I'll lay on an opening bombardment for six o'clock. We'll make it as noisy as possible. All the mortars and small arms, and they've got one pack howitzer they're just dying to use. I hope they know how to handle it."

Hugo looked at his watch. It was half-past one. He said, "Wake me at four o'clock."

"I believe there's a camp bed in the manager's office."

"I don't need a bed," said Hugo. "Six feet of floor and a blanket will do nicely."

The moment after he had shut his eyes, someone was shaking him by the arm. It was the sergeant, and he had a mug of coffee in one hand. He was still grinning. The prospect of fighting seemed to affect him that way.

"Fifteen minutes, we start," he said.

Hugo gulped the coffee down somehow. His stomach felt most peculiar; but more from his odd diet of the last two days than from apprehension. In fact, as the three trucks, with six policemen in each, rolled out of Mohara and up the coast road, his feelings were close to exhilaration. A light mist had crept inland from the saltings and had hidden the stars. The moon was down, and he could sense the approach of dawn.

"And gentlemen in England now abed," said Hugo softly.

"Wassat?" said Cowcroft, who was driving the leading truck, with Hugo in the passenger seat beside him.

"Nothing."

"We had patrols out during the night. They reported all clear as far as the Hammuz fork. In fact, they may have abandoned the palace and gone scuttling back into their hills."

"I hope not," said Hugo.

Crowcroft looked at him out of the corner of his eyes and said, "I hope not, too. I want them where I can see them. Dr. Kassim particularly."

"You think he's leading them now?"

"He's the only one with any real ideas. Alid's a creep."

They bowled on in silence for a time. They were past the side road to Hammuz now, and the mist was thinning. Apart from the beat of the engines and the humming of their tires on the wet tarmac, the silence was uncanny.

"There's a house on the right somewhere here," said Hugo. "A big white one with red tiles and a wall round it. We could leave the trucks there and go on foot."

"I know the one you mean," said Cowcroft. "It belongs to Ahmed Tuli, the banker."

"Then the Tuli bank is one I'm not patronizing," said Hugo. "Not if he's capable of leaving a dog tied up, to die of thirst."

"Arabs don't think about animals the way we do," said Cowcroft. He made a signal and the trucks behind closed up and followed them down the track to the Tuli house.

"Get them backed, ready to scarper if we have to," said Cowcroft. "We'll leave a driver with each. The rest come with us. And get a move on."

He looked up at the sky, which was now definitely whiter.

"It'll be all right," said Hugo. "We can keep out of sight of the palace most of the way. We may have to crawl the last bit."

The mist, which was still hanging round in the hollows, helped them. When Hugo lifted off the grating, Cowcroft crawled up beside him and peered down in horror.

"Do you mean we've got to go down that?"

"Right."

"But it's a drainpipe."

"I came up it, you can go down it."

"You might have warned me. I wouldn't have worn this uniform."

"Roll your trousers up above your knees."

"You mean . . . ?"

"*Above* your knees," said Hugo firmly.

It was easier, because Cowcroft had brought an electric torch, which they were able to use once they were safely inside the tunnel. The disadvantage was that the torchlight showed up the small creatures of the abyss which Hugo had only imagined before.

"Christ!" said Cowcroft. "How long does this go on? And stop that bloody noise."

The policemen seemed to be enjoying it.

"Once we're round this corner, we're back on dry land."

"We'd better wait there until the balloon goes up." The men squatted on the flagstones while Cowcroft consulted his watch. It was ten to six.

The next ten minutes were long ones. The chill of the underground passage had got into Hugo's bones. The secret of war was to keep moving. If you were running forward, or even if you were running backward, the movement anaesthetized you. Better still if you could make a noise. He realized now why savages screamed as they fought. Zulus, Pathans, Chinese pirates . . .

His head was nodding when he was jerked back to full awareness by a formidable explosion of sound.

"There's our cue," said Cowcroft. "Bang on time." He switched on his torch and they stumbled to their feet and set off down the passage. Behind them Hugo could hear the clicking of bolts as the policemen cocked their automatic rifles. He thrust his hand down the front of his shirt and pulled out the Luger. It was comfortably warm.

As they turned the last corner, the noise of battle rose to a climax. The ear-splitting crack of mortar bombs bursting in the confined space of the courtyard above their heads; the rattle of automatic fire; the thud and crump of a howitzer; men screaming.

Hugo climbed the steps that led up into the open air. Cowcroft's orders had been simple. Get out and start shooting. Shoot anything that moves. Then get the main gate open as quick as you bloody well can.

A man was standing, with his back to Hugo, under cover of the arched doorway. As he turned, Hugo recognized him. It was Dr. Kassim. He had a blood-stained rag tied round his forehead and a machine gun over one shoulder.

For a moment in time he stared incredulously at Hugo, then came at him, dragging one foot but coming fast, swinging the maching gun with the firing portion.

Hugo jerked up his Luger and pulled the trigger. Nothing happened. At the same instant that he realized he had forgotten to take off the safety catch, someone fired three times from behind him. Gouts of red appeared in the front of Dr. Kassim's robe, but it was going to take more than three bullets in his body to stop him.

He crashed into Hugo. They went down together. Light and sound were blotted out.

Chapter 23 / Dustpan and Brush

They had arranged Hugo's bed so that he could look out of the window. His apartment had been broken into, and looted twice. It was now a moderately tidy battlefield. Most of the mess had been cleared up, and some new furniture installed.

He was suffering from the aftereffects of severe concussion. The shake-up of his brain had been caused by hitting his head on the stone floor when he went down under the dying Dr. Kassim. His depression had causes which went deeper.

Out in the street he could see parties of American Marines perambulating along the waterfront. They were followed by a horsefly swarm of Umrani children. The small ones seemed to be begging for chewing gum, the older ones for cigarettes. Both lots were rewarded. Moharram was doing a roaring trade.

Hugo grunted and turned over in bed. He turned slowly because if he made any sudden movement, the room was apt to rotate alarmingly. Nawaf came in.

He said, "How are you feeling today, Mr. Greest?"

"Fine," said Hugo. "I'll be getting up tomorrow."

"That is good. I have a message for you, from the ruler. He would have wished to come and see you, to thank you for all that you did. But the Council thought it wiser that he should not pay private visits until the declaration of the coronation, and the public procession from the mosque here in Mohara."

"Quite right. When is the big day?"

"It is today."

"Today? Good heavens! That's a bit quick, isn't it? Three days isn't very long for a broken arm to set."

"Both the Council and His Highness were in agreement, however. In a country like Umran there can be no delay in acclaiming the ruler. In the ordinary way the coronation of the new ruler takes place before the sun goes down on the day of the old one's death."

"You know your business best, I imagine."

"Another thing," said Nawaf. There was a hint of embarrassment in his voice and Hugo half guessed what was coming. "This, too, is a decision of the Council and not of His Highness. They feel that in view of what has happened, an adviser on military matters must be chosen from among the Americans. Mr. Ringbolt has offered to fill the post temporarily, until a permanent official can be sent from the United States. It is their intention, I understand, to establish a trade delegation here."

"I see."

"To assist us in restoring the economy of our country."

When Nawaf said this, there was a very slight smile around the corners of his mouth. Hugo got the impression that if the Americans thought they were going to pocket the smitherite concession for chewing gum and cigarettes, they were in for a surprise.

"There is a further matter I ought to mention, since it may concern you personally. I fear that an accident may have occurred to a colleague of yours."

So much had happened in the last few days that it was only with an effort that Hugo gathered what Nawaf was talking about.

"Colonel Rex? I wondered why I hadn't heard from him. You say he has met with an accident?"

"I understand so. In Beirut."

"What sort of accident?"

"There is no certainty, but it seems very probable that he is dead. A woman of the town came under suspicion when she tried to change a number of dollar bills of large denominations. It transpired that Colonel Delmaison had been lodging with her. She was questioned, very closely. In the end some sort of account emerged. She had connections with the Janni brothers, who control much of the poppy market. It would be their people who did the actual killing, not the woman herself."

"I knew nothing of this."

"I am sure you did not."

"It's damned awkward, though. I suppose I shall have to go to Beirut and try to sort it out."

"There may be ways to arrange these matters. You must not trouble yourself about them while you are indisposed. I must go now. The procession leaves the mosque in five minutes."

"Then it was very good of you to come at all," said Hugo. He thought that the young king was lucky to have a man like Nawaf at his elbow. He was going to need him. He was going to need all the help he could get, with the Gulf sheiks pulling him in one direction and the Americans in the other. He was thinking about this when the door opened again and Robert Ringbolt looked in.

He said, "How's the invalid?"

"Fine," said Hugo. "I'm fine. Why aren't you taking part in the celebrations?"

"A planned absence was considered tactful. I saw Nawaf coming away. I take it he's put you wise to the general situation."

"He told me the U.S.A. had made a takeover bid. Rather ahead of your normal schedule, wasn't it? I seem to remember that the general plan was to let the fuzzy-wuzzies massacre each other and raise every sort of hell, before you came in with a dustpan and brush. Actually the situation was pretty well in hand when you landed."

"It was Tammy."

Hugo stared at him.

"Normally our tolerance parameters are pretty flexible. But when Admiral Grossberger learned that there was an American girl ashore, who might actually be in the hands of the natives, well, he just gave the orders to go right in."

"I see."

"Of course, he wasn't to know that she had you there to look after her."

205

"You're quite sure he was thinking about Tammy and not about the smitherite concession."

"Maybe he was thinking a bit about both," said Ringbolt with his disarmingly boyish smile. "I know just how you feel about this, Hugo, don't think I don't. However, I've got one proposition which may lift the clouds a piece, if you'd care to accept it. Those arms of yours—I guess they're pretty well stuck in Beirut at this moment. Now that the colonel has cashed in his chips—and between you and me, Hugo, not ahead of time—I imagine you're going to have some logistical problems when it comes to moving them on?"

"That's an understatement."

"Well, we've got a bit of pull in Beirut just now, politically and financially. We'd be happy to buy those arms off you and conclude the deal ourselves. I can't promise that you'd make all the profit you were planning on, but you'd get out with something on the credit side to make up for the fact that you're losing your assignment here."

"A golden handshake," said Hugo.

"I don't want to press it right now. Perhaps you'd like to think it over."

"No need to think it over. From now on, the arms are the property of the U.S. government."

"There'll be quite a few papers to sign. Fortunately we have a lawyer aboard with Admiral Grossberger."

"A very well-equipped fleet," said Hugo.

When Ringbolt had gone, the black depression descended on Hugo like a cloud clamping down onto a mountaintop. "Why do our people have to be so bloody feeble?" he said. "If they'd had the simple guts to move in a half battalion of infantry when I suggested it, we should have that concession in our pocket and billions of dollars a year. Napoleon called us a nation of shopkeepers. We're not even that now. We're retired shopkeepers, frightened to raise our voices in case we offend someone, frightened to move in case we tread on someone's toes."

"Talking to yourself," said Tammy. "That's bad."

She had come in quietly, and was sitting on the edge of the bed.

206

"Reaction," said Hugo.

"It was the same with me. As soon as I got back here I had a hot bath, and burst right out crying."

"I'm glad you're here, and not riding in that state carriage beside Hussein, bowing to the crowd."

"It was suggested. But I didn't feel able to accept." She looked at him out of the corner of her eye, a sliding sideways glance that was particularly her own, and said, "That policeman friend of yours. What's his name?"

"Martin Cowcroft."

"A nice little man. Just like a lizard. He told me he'd routed the procession to come right under your window. I think this is them coming now."

The crowd in the street had been thickening up steadily. Both pavements were packed. Small boys were running out into the road and being hauled back by their sisters. A police jeep drove past.

"Tammy," said Hugo. "Will you marry me?"

"Marry," said Tammy thoughtfully. "That's a bit old-fashioned, isn't it? A famous television star, a girl secret service ace. It's not what your viewers would expect."

"I'm an old-fashioned type," said Hugo. He slid one arm round Tammy, pulled her down on top of him, and started to kiss her.

The noise outside increased.

"Here they come," said Tammy. She spoke indistinctly.

"To hell with them," said Hugo. "I want you in this bed."

"Hold it one moment."

The noise rose to a climax. Motor engines, horns, bells, a clatter of hoofs, music, the screams of the crowd.

Hugo hoisted himself up, without letting go of Tammy, and looked out of the window. The open Rolls was turning the corner. Hussein was seated in the back, his left arm in a sling. When he looked up and saw Hugo, he half rose in his seat and waved his free arm. For a moment the solemnity of the occasion was lost, and he was an excited boy again.

For the last time in his life, thought Hugo, waving back vigorously and grinning.

The crowd roared its appreciation.

It took a week to clear things up. Ringbolt accepted the loss of his secretary philosophically, and gave them an advance wedding present of a case of Moharram's best champagne.

Martin Cowcroft and Charlie Wandyke came to the airport to see them off. Cowcroft said, "We're keeping our fingers crossed. You noticed that cousin Alid was in the procession. It looks as though they're patching up some sort of truce. It won't last, of course. We shall have trouble again as soon as the Yanks go. On the other hand, we should have the rest of the arms safely in by then."

As the plane rose from the runway and circled, Hugo saw the two men, suddenly diminished, waving good-bye. Although they could not possibly see him, he waved back. Good-bye, good-bye to Umran. Then they were out over the sea, transparent in the morning light, layer upon layer of gold and pink and light green and blue.

It was at Bahrain that it first became apparent that it was going to be no ordinary trip.

When Hugo started to move with the other passengers into the transit lounge, he and Tammy were asked to wait, and were then taken into VIP reception. Here they found a little crowd of newspapermen waiting for them. Hugo shook all the hands that were offered and caught a few names. It was not only the representatives of the local papers. The Middle East correspondent of the *Daily Telegraph* was there. Even more surprisingly, the *New York Times* seemed to have flown a man over simply for this encounter.

Hugo knew enough about the press to let them do most of the talking, and posed for a photograph with one arm round Tammy.

As they moved out again to the plane, one of the air hostesses directed them to the first-class section at the front of the plane. When they explained that they had economy-class tickets, the girl smiled sweetly and said, "That's O.K., Mr. Greest. The

208

airline has adjusted all that. Pleased to have you with us."

"What's all this about?" said Hugo. "How did those newspapermen know we were coming? Why the special treatment? What the hell's happening?"

"I guess it's something to do with my father," said Tammy.

"How does he come into it?"

"He has something to do with newspapers in the States."

"Tammy," said Hugo. "Stop evading the issue. What does your father do?"

"I don't think he does much. He's just a majority stockholder in one or two papers."

The desert of Arabia streamed below them and the hills of Beirut arose on the horizon. Hugo said, "Thank you," to the stewardess and accepted a glass of iced champagne.

By the time they reached Heath Row, he was unsurprised to find the press of London awaiting them, with its mouth wide open. By that time he was too full of airline food and airline drink to care. "Is it true, Mr. Greest, that you rescued the young prince yourself?"

"Well. Yes, I suppose I did."

"And Miss Biederbecker was with you in this cellar?"

"Miss who?"

"That's me," said Tammy.

"Certainly she was with me in the cellar. All the time."

"And this character you strangled with your bare hands?"

"Strangled?"

"The rebel chief."

"Actually, he was shot."

"You shot him, Mr. Greest?"

Hugo said, "I suppose I must have done."

Outside, in the streets, the placards were already on show.

TIGER WINS AMERICAN HEIRESS

REAL-LIFE DRAMA FOR SCREEN HERO

TV PERSONALITY IN MIDDLE EAST COUP

"We'd better get hold of a copy of that paper," said Hugo, "and find out what really happened."

Chapter 24 / The 92nd Tiger

Hugo's car was trapped behind a long line of cars, lorries, taxis, and buses, but mainly cars, driven by home-going businessmen who were wondering, for the hundredth time, whether it wouldn't have been more sensible to come up to town by train. There was fog ahead, and already the queues were beginning to build up on the motorways and the illuminated diversion signs were being switched on.

The driver, who was from the television studio pool, and knew that part of London like his own back garden, said, "Once we get past this road junction, I can slip off to the left and we can say good-bye to this crowd. We shall need a bit of luck at Chiswick, but I reckon it's worth it."

"I leave it to you," said Hugo. "We're in very good time. They can't start without me."

They were telerecording episode 92 that evening. "The Return of the Tiger." By popular demand, thought Hugo. No doubt about that. Had not the first person to telephone him when he got back to England been Sam? "They're falling over themselves to cash in on all this gorgeous publicity," he said. "I can sign you up for two more series of thirteen, with a one-way option on a third series. And listen, I think I can get you a percentage on the resale to America."

He had not been keen, but Tammy had overruled him. She said, "Take the cash. You can always quit at the end."

"Then do what? Live on my wife?"

"Why not? It's a comfortable sort of life, I imagine. I can't see why men object."

"We'll see about that," said Hugo. The conclusion of his arms deal with the American government had left him with enough money not to worry too much about the immediate future.

They jerked on a dozen yards and stopped again. It was warm in the car and Hugo turned down the side window, but this let in such a blast of freezing fog that he quickly shut it again.

There had been good moments and bad ones in the months since his return. The best had been his mother's reception of Tammy. They had got to terms immediately. His mother had said, "The real trouble with Hugo is that girls have tended to fall down and worship him. I'm sure you won't make that mistake."

"I'll fight against it," said Tammy gallantly.

After that they got straight on to discussing the wedding arrangements.

"As long as it isn't a show business wedding," said Mrs. Greest. "You know what I mean. Caxton Street Registry Office, crowds blocking the traffic, the bridegroom carrying the bride in his arms, and a funny man from the BBC cracking jokes on the pavement."

Tammy shuddered, and said, "Nothing like that. Technically I understand we ought to get married from my home. It's a place called Nantasket, and it has a very pretty little church with a white clapboard steeple."

In the end they had decided that this would be too complicated, and the wedding took place in Richmond Parish Church with a reception at the Star and Garter Hotel. Sam, of course, had come. And Hugo had, after some hesitation invited Raymond Taverner, who had returned a diplomatic refusal. The only disruption had been caused by the Tiger Fan Club, who had got into the reception ahead of the guests and taken away most of the wedding cake as souvenirs.

The car made thirty yards.

"Any minute now," said the driver.

The bad moments had mostly been regret for Umran. When the weather was particularly vile, he had thought about it a lot. The arch of the sky, deep blue above, fading to pearl on the horizon. The heat that pressed down on you like a weight, that hurt and anaesthetized the hurt at the same time, until in the end, like Martin Cowcroft, you lived in it and on it, a salamander in the fire. And the smell of musk and tamarisk and rotten fish and boiling tar, all mixed with the smell of the real desert, which was indescribable and which he had known when he was young.

That was the truth of the matter, he decided. It was a young man's land. When he had tried to explain this to Tammy, she had said, "To listen to you, anyone would think you were seventy. You've got more than half your life ahead of you. When this series is over, we'll go to America and I'll show you some *real* deserts. You could lose Arabia in some of them."

The car shook itself free of the traffic and bowled down a side street of small suburban houses. Front doors were opening, letting out a stream of light and letting in the breadwinners, home to a quiet evening of supper, television, and bed. They were his public. The ninety-nine point nine percent, who liked to live quietly and were happy to enjoy their excitements vicariously. Sensible people, who only knew vaguely where the Persian Gulf was, and had never heard of Umran.

They reached the television studios with half an hour to spare. Hugo signed six autograph books and stopped in the entrance hall for a word with George, the one-armed commissionaire.

"Very glad to see you back, Mr. Greest. My family always look forward to your show."

"Thank you, George. I hope we don't let you down."

"Very exciting, the first episode. Mr. Larrimore lent me the script. Very ingenious, I thought. Topical, too."

As the lift carried him skyward, Hugo pondered this. Episode one of the current series featured the kidnapping by terrorists of the home secretary's beautiful daughter. She was rescued from the terrorists by the Tiger at a moment when the government was on the point of giving way to their demands and releasing all the prisoners in Dartmoor.

It occurred to him that if life went on at its present rate, writers of this sort of stuff were going to have to run fast to keep up with it.

212